2016

South of Everything

South of Everything

A Novel

Audrey Taylor Gonzalez

Published 2015
Printed in the United States of America
ISBN: 978-1-63152-949-8
Library of Congress Control Number: 2015933360

For information, address:
She Writes Press
1563 Solano Ave #546
Berkeley, CA 94707

She Writes Press is a division of SparkPoint Studio, LLC.

I want to dedicate the book to my beloved friend, Ms. Deanie Parker, who has walked the road with me on this literary journey.

Preface

Old Thomas, Mammyrosy, Reddaddy, Annie Mae Oliver, Troy Finley, Nutie, and our beloved Georgiana Finley—some of them are characters in *South of Everything*, but they are also real people who taught me how to love, Jesus-style. They have met their maker and have no more sorrow or pain. But I never go a day without thinking of one or more of them. I've written this novel as a tribute to these angels who filled my home with gospel tune and prayer as they cared for me and my children, and maybe still do— and who placed solidly in me the cornerstone of my faith, without even knowing it.

I hope all my African American friends can read this novel without pain, as its only intention is love. Only love. It records the way things were in the 1940s and '50s, with apology for the bad parts— the disrespect—that still stumble around, nipping at justice's heels. I use the language that stays in my memory, because that is what was and we cannot wipe it out as if it never existed. Bear with me, because this is truth from a privileged young girl's point of view. It was real to her, though it came to good only when she was ordained, at fifty-six, to Holy Orders of the Anglican Episcopal Church in Uruguay.

The story is of a time that has gone, that doesn't exist anymore.

It was a time of innocence when we young'uns didn't know that what we were doing was degrading and awful, because it was the way things were. For a child, it was a time of learning about trust and creativity and vision. It was a time when a special young girl got acquainted with her spirit and her possibilities. This didn't necessarily come from her parents. It came from those around and behind, "the help," who took care of her without getting the credit.

It was a time before the social and political change in the early '40s, on the front end of freedom and the back end of slavery, when things were coming up that had to be done away with but weren't finished yet—and that's where I am taking you, reader, to know what it was like when a child begins to see the differences and discrepancies in life. For Missy Sara, it was a time of discovery of what was laid out before her, as she grew aware that things were not so rosy underneath as above.

I am weary of the cruelty and bitterness and injustice still proffered by my own race. I'm tired of jump-start conclusions and prejudices. I hate that children, who are so open and innocent and wanting to love and to give and to know, cannot because they are stuck in an environment where so many limits and so much hatred are instilled in them that they all grow in the wrong direction. We have to be careful that religion doesn't do that to us as well, make us all grow in one direction, as one trunk with no branches—because with no branches, there is no fruit.

There are lots of roads to God, and some of us have to go the long way, the rough way, the tragic way to get there, but God never told us that we couldn't or shouldn't or wouldn't. We must all be prodigal sons or daughters, and when I see these better-than-thou fundamentalists who get their spirituality by criticizing and condemning others, I am ashamed we are preaching the same Word.

And for now, with hopes I hug in my heart, I wait for that day when I can be with all these beloved people again and they will show me the green pastures where they have escaped pain, evil, and injustice, because God, in his abundant grace, has wiped it all away.

I
Lifting Up

One

~~~~

In West Tennessee God forgot his geography. Decades past an earthquake caused the Mississippi River to flow backward and form a lake called Reelfoot. That's all we got. No Smoky Mountains in this part of the state. No table-flat buttes. No skyscrapers. Only the Mississippi chewing its way along the border like an old timer working the tobacco stuffed in his gums. Settlements that imbibed the muddy juice along the river were about as tangy as the brown banks, and people seemed to want to keep it that way—quiet and out of harm's way, or covered if harm got in the way. Waiting for disaster. Fending it off by doing nothing.

Germantown, where our family lived, on the southeast side of Shelby County, carried on this pace, away from urban Memphis, near where Wolf River set free from the Mississippi. Germantown had less roll than the railroad tracks that passed through it, and the soil was poorer than the rich Delta lands below the riverbanks. The hills weren't as adamant in their lifting up as the rest of Tennessee, kind of like an illegitimate landscape born of its neighbor states but cut out because it had to be somewhere to hold up all those trees, Herefords, hogs, horses, cotton bales, and unpainted sharecropper houses. Farms backed into each other. Only tornado warnings twirling over from Arkansas charged up the atmosphere, but no one panicked, trusting in the famous Memphis bluffs, humps of hills along the river that old-timers swore clipped the tornado's tail so it jumped over Shelby County.

This was dull country out here, unpestered by progress. Still safe. People behaved. Everyone knew his place, his role in a situation. Nothing much went on, and if it did, everyone knew about it. Germantown was not a town of Germans. In fact, it changed its name to Nashoba during the World War. Nashoba was an old Indian name for "wolf", probably Chickasaw. But this wasn't a town of Indians either. What did we know of Indians? Indians lived out West and held rain dances, wore feathers and moccasins, and showed up in Lone Ranger comic books as villains. When I was ten I got a crush on an Indian, a wrangler at a dude ranch out in Colorado where our family went summers. Neal Ride the Wind, he was, with long black hair under his Stetson, every strand in place as if just brushed, moving like a curtain over his lemon-colored slicker as he brought up the guests' horses. Back then I was just a pudgy nuisance who could sit a horse pretty well, Western shirt barely snapping across my jelly-roll midriff, shapeless jeans, cuffs turned up off the ground.

But home was Germantown, and in the '40s, when I grew up there, Germantown was Deep South, not Indian Country—but an uneventful, unincorporated town of insignificant people, tractors taking up half the narrow roads, big farms, rolling grass every whichaway, a "for whites only" county high school with yellow buses, plenty of wood shacks and barns, and a few stately old homes left over from pre–Civil War fancy. There were probably more colored people than white living in the country. Rich white folks had big houses mostly in town. On plantations the houses were colonial style, with portico porches from which there was a view, while colored people had unpainted porches lifted off the ground by bricks stacked under the four corners to keep out floodwater and rats. Hound dogs and sneaky snakes slept under the crooked open-air porches, unraveling screen doors banged listlessly in the breeze, and early Maytag washers rested in the front yard. Hound dogs welcomed visitors, their heads drooped knee level, anticipating an ear-pull. They howled if you played on a piano.

Poor white folks lived like that, too, people like Mr. Hugh and his family, who took care of the cows on our farm. Sons had BB guns and played football, tinkered with dead automobiles, and took girlfriends over the state line to Hernando, Mississippi, to get married. B-Budd Hugh was one of my first friends.

We lived in one of those big houses, and we knew colored people better than most because they lived next to or with us on our farms. The farm men got up at dawn, hooked up the mules, drove the feed from pasture to pasture no matter if there was rain or sleet or snow, sort of like the postman. The women rocked us from the cradle and arranged us for getting married and cooked the biscuits Daddy wanted every night for dinner. The men wore white coats to serve dinner, and the women washed and folded our delicate underwear and changed the sheets every other day. They inherited our unwanted clothes and broken toys—not the fine things, which Mother sent to the Junior League. Their children conspired with us to throw baby pigs out of haylofts to see if they bounced and then fled with us from the angry farm manager so as not to get killed. They galloped bareback with us on the walking horse and played war with us by the old ponies in the pastures.

They called me Missy Sara, and they called my brother Master Robertelee, even when we were children. Never first names alone. Daddy called them "the help," and Mother called them "the servants." From childhood I guessed they were ours because they were always there, polishing up the house so it was a showpiece. When I was two and three, I knew if I stood at the top of the stairs and yelled, "Yeh-Yeh, come get me," the butler whose name was Willie would soon have me up in his arms and tote me to the bottom of the stairs.

Like the servants at the big house, where things were nicer, the farm help's life seemed to begin and end where they worked. The old men hardly scattered from the farm because it was a long walk to anywhere, and weekends they walked to church or to a mule race where they could win silver dollars, or maybe they'd go down to Hoppers' for fried chitlins and marshmallowed sweet potatoes, which kind Mrs. Hoppers prepared with great skill.

Old men poked along on foot at the edge of rut-filled Stout Road, ambling in slow motion, dark apparitions dressed in layers of caramel brown or parson black, even on the hottest days, often a thick stick in hand, a tow sack over the shoulder, a hat on the head, going to or coming from in the same manner so the foot-paths were worn like cattle trails. The kids rode thin bicycles or an unkempt pony.

But before the farm, when I was six and we still lived at my grandfather Reddaddy's mansion on South Parkway, I dressed in my favorite pink pinafore with the bibbed front that barely covered my chubby chest one Easter morning and waited impatiently for Mother to get ready for church. She was taking a long time, so I went out to the barnyard, where our twin goats, Custard and Pudding, lived with my Shetland pony, Penny. When I walked in, Penny, her teeth almost as big as her hooves, gave my shoulder a nip, and then she shook her head with its golden mane and reared up to put her hooves on the fence. A loud whinny and a few nose blows, and she stood on her hind legs for a few seconds before going back down. She did that only for me. I knew she was a trick pony because of that. But no one believed me when I told them. For my birthday parties Penny, on her best behavior, was hitched to the six-seat wicker cart to give my guests with balloons tied to their wrists a ride around the front driveway. Most of the time I wasn't allowed to ride her unless Old Thomas wasn't busy. I was only allowed to feed her sugar cubes, which she nudged off my flat hand. So I wanted to go find Thomas. I thought he must be picking strawberries for our cook Mammyrosy's shortcake, but before I could, Mother yelled for me to come get in the car.

I turned and ran toward her call, and that's when I tripped and fell hard on the gravel driveway. The hurt wasn't too awful, but three rocks stuck in my knee. I cried, and when I got to the car, I told Mother what had happened. She didn't believe I was wounded. No one did, because no one could see the rocks lodged under the skin and my knee wasn't bleeding. Besides, we were late, and Mother was in a big rush to get us to Sunday school, so she ordered me to quit fussing and get in the car.

When I told Robertelee about the rocks he said if I kissed my knee, they would go away. So that day when we got home I looked at my knee in the mirror and watched those rocks glistening deep under the skin. I realized there was no way I could kiss my knee. I could only push my finger in and out on the triangle. Those rocks felt like hard candy in the bottom of my Christmas stocking. Day after day I studied them and pushed at them, and when I was fiddling with the rocks, I'd get a fizzy sensation that I was being lifted up.

At that age I didn't know if it was magical or spiritual or what that sensation was. I couldn't evaluate it then. But I promise you, this is true: when no one was around, I could fiddle with those rocks and then I could float down the grand curving staircase of the big house. If I whispered, "Lift me up, Lord," He'd do it. He'd lift me up. I could think where I wanted to be, and a moment later I'd be there. At the top of the grand front steps, my feet would hover a shoe's length off the first step and I'd drift slowly, in vertical fashion, from the top step to the safety of the bottom one. The sensation felt as smooth and delicious as ice-skating on a cold day.

Sometimes in the night, while I slept with my cat Flossie, the rocks in my knees stung, and I was sure the bogeyman was chewing on my toes. I didn't want to look to see if he was. If my covers were on, I was safe and the bogeyman would get bored and go bother my brother in his room. But during restless nights, a scary dream began in me. In that same pink pinafore and with my rock-filled knee leaking blood, I had to run in curves around the tall oak trees as I tried to dodge red Chevrolets aiming to run directly over me. I hid behind the thinner elms or turned sharply in narrow triangles around the poplars, feeling wise that I knew metal cars couldn't bend around trees, and then, exhausted, I stretched out on the ground as flat as possible in my roundness, so wheels could pass by on either side of my body without the belly of the car scraping my stomach.

Of course, I didn't tell anyone except Old Thomas about these things. Old Thomas was the colored man my grandfather Reddaddy had brought up from one of the cotton warehouses, and he was magical. He could analyze just about anything. Old Thomas knew so many stories I just wanted to be around him all the time. He knew that the inside of people didn't always tell the outside. Many people came to him for advice. He never admitted to any powers because once the police hauled him off, and he didn't want that to happen again. Maybe he really was a healing man, but he just wouldn't practice on people who particularly wanted to be practiced on. He practiced on whatever was closest at hand. Old Thomas had a special way with animals, especially those with religious potential. He taught a dozen pink and black pigs how to pray before they dove into their evening meal, and he taught chickens how to squat down over their legs for an epistle reading and sit still until it was over, and dogs wandered along behind him so that he might have picked up a whole congregation of them by the time he got a short piece down the road. Mother thought it was strange how the dogs that usually try to bite colored people loved Old Thomas. Maybe it was because he hummed like an icebox or a summer ceiling fan. When things were quiet, it was the hum you picked up. Old Thomas even hummed when he was serving and it wasn't proper to speak, like at dinner when he passed the lady peas mounded up in silver dishes. It bothered my mother to have to put up with his humming. But she couldn't get rid of Old Thomas because Reddaddy had made an agreement with Daddy that Old Thomas would be there with us all his life. And that he'd be safe. Daddy knew some secrets that Mother didn't, so she simmered a bit in being left out. "Thomas is doing that humming stuff again," she'd complain, returning from the kitchen to the den, where the sound of Vaughn Monroe came out of the record player. She'd be hoping to get sympathy from Daddy, who kept his eyes focused on the Zane Grey western he was reading.

"Whenever he gets like that, nothing gets done," Mother said into space. She was never satisfied with "the help," even though most stayed with us until death. And she had no patience with burning religion. If anyone got religious inspiration during work hours, it stirred her nerves.

"Is he going into a trance again?" Mother asked Mammyrosy, who was beating the cream for prune whip.

"Dunno, Miz Lucy," Mammyrosy replied, the muscles in her walloping arm like knots in a seaman's rope. Mammyrosy wasn't getting into anybody's debt. She had a tendency to nap when Old Thomas hummed, and when dinner was all ready to be served, the turnip greens and corn pudding and squash casserole pierced at right angles by the oversize serving spoons so Mother would have no problems with the first serving, Mammyrosy rested in her metal chair in the corner and fell asleep sitting up. Automatically at 6:00 p.m. her eyes snapped open, and Old Thomas would quell his humming and go announce that dinner was served.

Now and then Mammyrosy wore a long white cotton dress and white beret to work; this outfit signified that she was going to the meeting of her Salvation Sisters group at the Coloreds Methodist Episcopal Church after she tidied up. Mammyrosy, too, had "experiences" with the Lord, but they were quieter than Old Thomas's and pretty much hers alone. When she got into a state of vision, she'd just close her eyes and beat whatever batter she was mixing even faster.

"I don't know why you all have to do these things right at dinnertime," Mother mumbled, pushing out the swinging door as she left the kitchen.

I figured Mother was disturbed that she couldn't order around the time and place of Jesus's activities, which seemed to have a priority around dinnertime. Or maybe she was disturbed because Old Thomas had a white eye that had been turning whiter and whiter lately and looked like the star opal one of Daddy's friends brought back from the war in India. You never knew where Old Thomas was looking, but he could see clearer than a dog's scent, and I always knew when he was looking at me, because when he was, I felt warm.

Even before I told him, Old Thomas knew things. I often passed my secrets on to him. He could spot a miracle from any distance and tell if it was real or fake, and when I told him about the dream, he claimed it had something to do with those rocks in my knee. He said my knee had snagged the three spots off the devil's dice, the kind we used playing board games but a more powerful version because they were red with brown spots. I couldn't figure out what the devil's red dice were doing in my grandfather's gravel driveway. Old Thomas didn't go into detail. But he did promise one day the devil would get his comeuppance and wouldn't win any more games.

On Sundays the population of Germantown swelled with Sunday drivers from Memphis looking for an outing or a good barbecue sandwich, because Germantown was home to the best barbecue pit in the country. Bozos, it was called, ten miles down Highway 61 from our farm. Barbecue lovers drove the twenty miles out of town for good pulled-pork barbecue sandwiches and a slab of ribs. Barbecue was born out of a way to make cheap, fatty meat edible, complimenting the laid-back lifestyle of these parts. Slide a pig's thigh on an iron grate, turn it every now and then, slop it with a sauce that stung with vinegar. This land I came from was a land where violence was turned deep into the soil, but no one dared bring it up except in whispers at Bozos. Bozos was an enigma. Besides being home to the best barbecue in the country, it was also its own sort of church where ideas got disturbed in conversation. Pull open the door, and be assured your spirit would soon be saved.

Two aged sisters, Miss Irma and Miss Lulu, with overbleached blond hair and aqua-blue eye shadow, ran Bozos on an old family recipe, a secret they planned to take to the grave with them, so we had to eat it while we could. Miss Irma looked like she was the barbecue taster, big and buxom in her spotty white apron over a flowered dress, and Miss Lulu was skinny. She always wore a green bow in her hair and green socks with her sandals because they matched her green apron with its big pockets. My Reddaddy went to Bozos so much he should have owned the place, and some days Old Thomas went along to visit with the sisters, too. But Reddaddy and County Sheriff Ferget met there every week, and sometimes on Sundays when Reddaddy could sneak away from the big house. For me it was the forbidden place I had to get to. Mother got upset when Reddaddy took me there and fed me pork barbecue. Pork was unkempt for a proper young girl, she said. And all that sauce, too messy for good manners. But besides the Lolololo tree, Bozos was one of my favorite places in the world, and Old Thomas and Reddaddy were my favorite people.

Two

―――

Most of the adventures of my youth happened in the back pasture of Wild Grass Farm. It stood out for its white fences, six boards each panel, that lined the pastures for miles and miles. In those years we were probably the only ones in Germantown who could afford the paint to have so much fence, and the white brick horse barn as long as a train tunnel. The stalls were so large they could house the Budweiser Clydesdale horses and have space left over. And best of all, on that farm was the tree way out in the back pasture. Old Thomas showed it to me and Robertelee, and right away we knew it was special. It was a tree that put doubts in you right away whether it really was a tree. Could have dropped out of the sky. Could have come up from China, which, we were told, was below us on the other side of the world. It was not an ordinary tree. It didn't fit a name. But whenever we were there, it shimmered with life and stood as tall as a smokestack with white smoke rings formed by clouds surrounding the top. When we walked away a few feet to leave it for a while, it was invisible. It didn't even peek above the weeds and the footprints of our arrival path disappeared. Without Old Thomas, we couldn't even find it.

Old Thomas called his magical tree the Lolololo.

Robertelee, being quite a bit younger than me, didn't understand mystery. Whenever we went out to the tree he just went along to play cowboys or swords or to squash bugs, and if he even saw what I saw, he didn't analyze it as odd or magical. But it was different for me. I could tell you a thousand tales that came from that tree, tales so odd it would disturb the mind of the sane. You wouldn't believe a word of it, but to me that tree was the most real thing in my life. It was wiser than teachers and priests and parents. When you looked at that tree, stories came at you like crystal chips fractured in a strange kaleidoscope. When you peeked through the turning hole, you could not stop looking because there was so much curiosity, so many stories born out of gesticulating stones. It harbored a whole zoo of animals inside it, and on the leafless branches Old Thomas hung straw baskets and built hay nests for wounded birds who could stay there while healing. And there were underground quarters for snakes who could slide in through O-holes to escape the sun. Old Thomas stroked those snakes and talked to them in a hum.

"What's 'Lolololo' mean, Old Thomas?" I asked. He didn't answer in answer style. He just hummed *lalalalololalolalolalo* without making much noise. Nothing could explain it. There was no other tree of miracles and visions on Earth like it. And Old Thomas said his instinct for snake helping came from his heritage in Africa, where snakes were treated with respect.

On humid summer days, whenever we ate dinner on the screened-in porch, Daddy swatted irritating flies with a flyswatter. When he got one, he'd say, "And another redskin hit the dust," and Robertelee and I would giggle. Daddy seemed to enjoy his fly kill, but he wouldn't kill anything else. Not even a quail in hunting season. And then, after dinner was served, Old Thomas, still in his white serving jacket, a broom and scoop in hand, went out to the porch and gathered up the dead fly bodies and put them in a tiny flower-printed cotton sack, a sack like women used for collecting smells. The corpse of a big fat horsefly was particularly rewarding. Then afterward he'd carry them to the Lolololo for his snake visitors, who considered them candy.

The Lolololo had a trunk so fat we didn't have a measuring tape on the farm that'd fit around it. The bark was practically white and generally smooth, but growing straight on the trunk were tiny red stems like painted fingernails. Old Thomas called these "beechos." I never knew if they were bugs or baby buds. Occasionally he'd rub his hand gently over the bark and end up with a pile of beechos in his hands, and he'd reserve these in his pocket to take out to Bozos. "Beechos is good eating," Old Thomas said, and for that day the bark of the Lolololo tree would be absolutely smooth. But when we returned the next day or the next, new little red stems would have popped up.

I never saw beechos anywhere else, and over the years, the Lolololo tree lost most of its branches, if it ever had them in the first place. What was left, trunk and branches, formed a cross, and in the armpits of the cross were pink and white leaves like giant four-leaf clovers, each petal indented with a reddish-brown spot. Fingering a leaf like a new note, Old Thomas said, "These dog leaves carry on dem petals the very memory of Jesus. See those spots of blood? They come from his feet and hands and head. The Lolololo sympathizes because Jesus hung on one of its brother dog trees on the mount of Golgotha."

Old Thomas just plain understood dog leaves. He collected them and dried the flattened shapes out in a hammock contraption strung between two old, useless fence posts where the sun could get at them. When all the life juice had been sunburned out, the leaves became not shriveled-up knots like raisins, but smooth, white communion wafers that looked like the flat four-petaled flowers I drew in kindergarten. And even though you won't believe this, Old Thomas said that on portentous days he'd break up the dog leaves to sprinkle into his barbecue sauce, the special one he prepared with Miss Lula and Miss Irma. Old Thomas's dog leaves mixed with the sisters' secretly marinated beechos was offered up at Bozos only on Sundays and only to Old Thomas's brothers and sisters of salvation after a particularly powerful church meeting full of hollering, chanting, and conversations with the Holy Ghost. Especially if someone had been lifted up in feeling the Lord's presence.

"For then the heavens will open up with a mighty chorus of angels," Old Thomas explained to me. I could see he was elated, satisfied in his assurance, his voice soft and firm, his eyes closed like window shades. "The Lord loves lifting up spirits."

In the big house, upstairs, overlooking the pastures and the magnolia trees, Mother had a dressing room separate from her bedroom and bath. Every afternoon about four o'clock she sat in that room, getting ready for Daddy's arrival home from the office. It was one of those places she often said to me, "Don't bother me now. I'm getting fixed up for Daddy," and she'd always change her shoes and put on her highest heels. One day, as she was puffing powder on her high cheekbones, I walked in and asked her what a portentous day was. She said she didn't know, and she asked me where I'd heard that word.

I didn't want to tell her about Old Thomas and the beechos, so I just said, "Oh, nowhere. It just came up in my mind," and I thought about running out of there. There were lots of doors for different reasons at our house—it was a big white house, with wings and columns and a portico porch for looking across all the land Daddy owned.

"You sound just like the servants," Mother said. "I don't know why we pay to send you to private schools if you haven't learned to talk any better than that." She was having trouble drawing on her lipstick and dealing with me at the same time, but I was glad for the distraction.

Robertelee and I never told Mother when we were going to the back pasture, or even that we went there at all. Still, I knew she had an inkling that when we weren't in the house, we were following Old Thomas around, just like Reddaddy's hound dog, Frightnin', did, and she always asked why in the world we followed him around. She'd say, "It's downright embarrassing," and I always answered her the same way when she said that. "Just because," I'd say, because back then I didn't really know why myself. I just knew I wanted to.

"I think you've been reading too many Richard Halliburton books," Mother said just as I ran out of the room. Richard Halliburton was an adventurer from Memphis who copied George Mallory, a man who got killed climbing Mount Everest; he copied brave people like Amelia Earhart and Lowell Thomas, too. I loved his books, but Mother hoped I wasn't planning to be an adventuress.

I always told her I just might, and sometimes, when she wasn't looking, I set her high-heeled shoes up in a row, like I set up my Madame Alexander dolls, and hoped I wouldn't have to wear Mother's shoes when I got older. I thought I'd rather be a nun and heal lepers in Africa like Audrey Hepburn did in *The Nun's Story*, a movie I'd watched with Daddy—and that I loved.

I also thought I was old enough not to always need permission to do things on the farm, so I kept things from Mother. Besides, she was usually at the Junior League doing volunteer service or at the country club playing tennis. Mammyrosy kept her notified of where we were except when we were at the Lolololo tree, because we didn't tell Mammyrosy when we went there either. Oh, from the upstairs window in the big house Mother could see the back pasture, but she never spoke about a tree out there. I guessed when she saw us running through the pastures, she assumed we were going to our secret hideout in the yearling pasture near the front of the farm, where a grove of pine trees surrounded a gully like useless columns on a temple ruin.

Sometimes I'd go there and make house layouts with sticks and invent furniture from pine needles and cones. I'd pretend to be married with children, even though I had to play alone. Sometimes green snakes visited and I rested pennies on their backs. They'd carry them, like waiters, from one room to the other. If I was caught where I wasn't supposed to be, I ended up being spanked by Daddy for making unwise decisions, but that didn't stop me from doing it again.

Three

There was one thing for sure: we did have some strange people on our farm. Daddy had to hire the most difficult workers because no one else would have them and Reddaddy would feel sorry for them and insist they work on Wild Grass Farm. That's how they found Mr. Hugh.

Mr. Hugh was mean. Cows liked him, but not much else did. He wasn't friendly with anyone, like he had something to hide and was afraid someone would catch him at it if he gave them more than a couple minutes of his time. I think Mr. Hugh hated everything except T-Royal Rupert the Forty-Ninth, Reddaddy's prize bull, the one he purchased at a cattle auction. T-Royal was big and fat, with curly red-and-white hair and polled horns rounded off so they wouldn't spear someone to death. When Mr. Hugh talked about that bull, he lit up like a streetlight, and Reddaddy always said it was T-Royal that lured Mr. Hugh to the farm. He had raised that bull from a calf and wouldn't part from it, so before he knew how Mr. Hugh behaved, Reddaddy asked him to come manage the cattle he and Daddy were accumulating.

Since Mr. Hugh was in charge of the whole herd of Hereford cattle at Wild Grass Farm, his family got to live in the manager's white clapboard house down by the front gate of the farm. It was that house we passed whenever we drove the long drive, past the barns and pastures, all the way up to the big house. My brother and I weren't allowed to go farther inside Mr. Hugh's house than that front porch, because he didn't like us children to be around. On hot days he let us sit on the porch to keep away from the stingers, and that's where we played with his boys, B-Budd and his little brother, Bummer. I think Bummer's real name was Drummond, but I was never sure. All I knew was that something was wrong with him, because he couldn't walk like other kids his age.

But Robertelee and I were drawn to B-Budd, especially because he raised rabbits: white ones, gray ones, blue ones, brown ones, speckled ones, bunches of them crowded up like fur muffs in corners of cages atop tall wooden legs. I loved to punch my fingers through the chicken wire and touch their fuzz. Their long ears lay flat on their backs, and their noses jerked up and down like they itched and couldn't scratch. B-Budd sold their skins for money. When the skins were peeled off, they got stiff like tree bark, and on the underside was a map of blood veins. I never could figure out why B-Budd wanted to kill them, but he said rabbit was good eating and profitable enough that he could go down to Hopper's General Store and buy firecrackers and licorice strings with the money he earned.

B-Budd also collected insects. He stored most of them in canning jars, which he set on his windowsills so they'd get the light. We could see those jars from the outside, filled with bodies of dead things, but we couldn't touch them. B-Budd was protective about his collection, particularly the wasps. He called those stingers. We had been told to stay away from stingers because they were just plumb mean, but B-Budd talked about them as if they were heroes, and they definitely loved B-Budd's house. In its corners, under rain gutters that hung off the roof's rim, stingers built nests as big as the tops of garbage cans. We had to duck as they took off from those nests in swarms and whizzed around the house in giant circles, making a noise like stock cars in a race. They went so fast it seemed if one hit you in the head, it might make a dent. So we had to be alert and know when to duck. Bummer had a big red ring on the side of his head where an oversize stinger dived on him and knocked him crazy. At least that's what B-Budd told us. He said that ever since then Bummer wouldn't eat anything but finger bread.

So B-Budd's revenge was to collect dead bodies of wasps, hornets, dirt dobbers, fat bumblebees, and yellow jackets. He stretched out and stabbed the stingers' bodies with nails against cardboard so he could study them. If he didn't find any new ones for a while, he took out the fly sprayer and pumped out something that'd kill a gang of them. Then, with his fingers, he'd pick them up off the ground when they were still flapping their little wings and drop them in those jars with others of the same type until they died. The biggest bodies B-Budd organized into a display, like a soldier hanging up his medals for all to see. When he had them ready, he explained to us where the stinging parts were. Once, little Bummer got into the display and tore a bunch of stingers off the cardboard, and B-Budd was so mad he crunched them to dust in his hand. But he never said a word to Bummer.

"Now don't you chilluns go down to that pond, Missy," Mammyrosy would say as my brother and I wandered out the back door of the big house with not much direction. She just knew where we were going. She had eyes like Elastic Man had arms. "That pond is full of snakes just waiting to grab yo socks," she'd add as she turned her back around to resume cooking. "Don't you know snakes snatch cotton socks so they have warm jackets for the winter?"

Mammyrosy laughed at herself. "Now, don't you go down there with Master Bubb either. He has no business killing those frogs. He won't eat 'em, so it's a whole waste of time. He just hurts those poor things and throws them back in the water to die. Such a cruel child. He sho is a cruel child."

But Robertelee and I didn't listen. The farm was big, and it took a good walk to get from one place to the other. The pond was about a mile down the driveway from the big house, right next to the horse barn that was filled with fine saddle horses. My brother and I rode bicycles because the big house was so far back into the farm it required a good effort to get down there. I think my daddy liked having so far to drive to get to the big house, because it gave him thinking time.

Of course we knew the pond was dangerous. All sorts of evil creatures held up under its murky surface: diamondback cottonmouths with white witches' teeth, thin silver copperheads that snuck up into the horse stalls in the barn and could kill you in a bite, blue racers that ran loose and fast, and skinny green garden snakes that didn't hurt anybody. They all hid in the mud under the water or in the crevices formed by leaves and green things. In fact, the pond was so choked with lily pads that huge snapping turtles could walk across and not sink. Old Thomas said if a snapping turtle bit us, he'd hold on until the sky thundered, and that always scared me enough to be careful not to fall in. There were so many places that looked flat and solid, but there wasn't anything there when you stepped on it. All the while, you had to keep an eye on the dirt dobbers and dragonflies continually swirling overhead, dipping down quickly to touch something and then soaring back up on its side like a warplane in the *Movietone News*.

B-Budd frog-gigged at the pond, and Robertelee and I raced our bicycles down there to watch, especially in the late fall when the weather was fine and the sky not too dark, right before dinnertime. B-Budd was down there with a stick. I asked him where he got it. He had to lay down the BB gun that was constantly under his arm so he could hold the flashlight in his left hand to see the frogs.

"Ohhh, I picked it up," he said.

"Where? Can I have one?"

"Nope. Girls don't frog-gig," he told me, so I had to just watch.

Frog-giggers stick wide metal forks in the end of long bamboo fishing poles to help them keep a distance from their prey. I don't think it escapes any frog when a human is making a sneak attack. They may not move fast enough, but they aren't dumb. When they'd hop off so the gig missed, B-Budd always mumbled, "Dumb frog."

He stood pretty far from the water and flashed his light around the pond's edges until a beam reflected on a frog's shiny skin. Then he hurled that stick like a spear. If the frog was sleeping and unsuspecting, the fork landed one prong on each side of its neck and held it there until the gigger could pick it up. If it was a bad throw, there'd be blood spurting everywhere. When B-Budd missed, he said it was just practice and regrouped for the next hurl.

He squatted down low and swam his flashlight across the pond, looking for a shine, and I whispered so he couldn't hear, "Jump, little froggies, jump; don't let him see your skin flash."

But the gig spear rushed through the air at whatever B-Budd had seen and pierced the back leg of a little frog trying to get out of its way. B-Budd pulled the stick back and took off the froggie, whose leg was attached, and threw him back in the pond.

"That one's too small to amount to something," he commented.

I swatted the horseflies arriving now that the horses had been turned out of their stalls and into the pastures, and I suggested he move closer so he wouldn't hurt the frogs.

"Let me tell ya, Missy." B-Budd drew up tall, reloading for another gig with a couple of practice thrusts. "When you see that shine picking up the light, you can't tell right off if it's a frog or a snake. I gotta take precautions. I gotta kill me some frogs, not a whole ballywack of snakes. God likes me capturing frogs. Back in olden days, God used them frogs to punish Eee-gyptians. Frogs were everywhere," he mumbled.

"Eee-gyptians?" I asked.

B-Budd had to swat a horsefly off the front of his face. "And horseflies, too. The Lord sent horseflies to eat them Eee-gyptians up," he mumbled with his back turned.

"It's not how big the kills is," he explained. "It's how many. Frogs ain't enough to fill a stomach. Ain't many of us put those things on the stove. Those France people do, though." B-Budd usually threw most of what he caught back into the pond.

Snakes, disturbed by the activity, lifted their snouts just above the waterline. In the next hurl, B-Budd gigged a cottonmouth by accident and I jumped back, but he dragged the squirming snake out and over the leaves, closer to him. I was yelling at him not to touch it, but that just made him get closer and braver while Robertelee ran to the grass where his tricycle was parked.

B-Budd dropped his gear and grabbed hold of that snake, one hand on its head, the other closer to its tail. Then he stretched it out and measured its length against his arm. I kept turning my head, then peeking back in a squint. I was sure the snake would snap back in a curl, but I had to admit I was impressed with B-Budd's bravery, and he kept on, practically choking that snake to death by forcing its mouth open and holding it up before his eyes so he could look right into its face and see those ugly, jagged teeth.

"They shall take up serpents," he shouted, lifting his catch high over his head. "And the Holy Ghost will move upon them." The snake kept squirming, but B-Budd laughed and said, "See, Missy, this serpent ain't thinking to bite me, 'cause he knows I'm saved," and he thrust it toward me and starting to yell out one of those psalms he came up with now and then. "Them church elders'll be proud," he said. "I'm young to be handling snakes."

I stepped slowly away from him, but I wanted to know, so I asked him.

"How do you get snakes to come to church, B-Budd?"

"They just arrives," he said, and then, inspired, he went on. "Sometimes rattler snakes done got hauled up from Texas when we've got a real powerful healing service coming up. You know, like when there's a bunch of cripples that need to walk. Girl, snake handlin' is sign of a real religious man."

Robertelee was riding his tricycle around in a circle at a good distance, but I still had a lot of questions.

"How does a snake know about religion?" I asked.

"A snake knows. He don't bite no righteous man. If you ain't been saved by the Lord Jesus Christ, and a snake bites, you gonna die faster than a pea rolls off a knife."

Then B-Budd flipped the cottonmouth like he would a boomerang back toward the other side of the pond. It landed with an enormous splash, and B-Budd began to gather up his gear. He tucked his shotgun under his arm. "It's getting late. You kids better get back to the big house," he said.

Then he stopped, moved close, and looked at me hard. "Missy, I have one thing to ask ya."

I had a hard time staring into his blue eyes, but I couldn't stop it, and for a minute I wondered if he'd have to be my boyfriend.

"What is it, B-Budd?" I sort of regurgitated out the words, and he put his hand on my shoulder and gave it a squeeze.

"Have you been saved?" he asked, without moving off his hand.

"Saved from what?"

"From sin, Missy. From sin," he said. His face looked serious in the dim light, and I couldn't stop looking. "I think you is righteous, Missy, but you've gotta be saved by the Lord or it don't count."

I didn't dare ask him what "righteous" was, or "sin," but I wanted to get out of there, so I told him I had to ask Mother, and I yanked myself away from him and ran to follow Robertelee back home.

Four

Mammyrosy didn't like my going down to Mr. Hugh's house, not for any reason. "A house occupied by dem stingers is an evil place," she said. "A house with stingers ain't the settling-in place of good people. Dey comes from another kind of creation, jest wanting to stir up trouble."

I never saw any stingers living around our house or Mammyrosy's house and definitely not around Old Thomas's. If one or two came around and got shut in our house, they buzzed loudly because they were eager to get out and go back home. Mammyrosy got really upset if any kind of flying bug got in her kitchen, and whenever that did happen, Old Thomas had to come all the way up from the shed that was a long way away from the big house—out near the barn—and get rid of it before she'd continue cooking. She was particularly smart on the subject of stingers because she said if one stung her, she'd die.

At Mr. Hugh's house, pretty soon after summer heated up, he set out to get rid of those stingers. With great ceremony, he threw hot black tar over their nests. "Hot tar'll run them off like a postman chased by a dog," he mumbled. For a while the whole place smelled like road repair, and B-Budd finished up the job by shooting BBs into the tarred holes to kill the stingers that hadn't escaped or were holding on for dear life.

When the tar hardened, Mr. Hugh knocked the nests down like he'd won a war, and he talked like he'd gotten rid of those old coots for good, but no matter what Mr. Hugh and B-Budd did, the very next summer stinger families returned to those very same corners and rebuilt those very same nests and took up buzzing around that house just as fast, and I was sort of glad because I thought trying to kill them was a cruel thing to do.

One day as Mother drove us through the front gate coming home from school, she glanced over at Mr. Hugh's house and suddenly said, "Oh my Lord, what's happened here!" But before we could look, she said, "Don't you look. Turn your heads the other way. I mean it!"

Naturally, we looked. There were ambulances and sheriff cars with the red lights on top, and people running back and forth, and a strange white truck parked with its back door open, in front of the house. As we drove past, I peeked inside the truck and saw it was filled with white bed pads, and three monster men in white were stuffing B-Budd inside. He was tied up in a white shirt that forced him to cross his arms like he was hugging himself, and I could see he couldn't get out of that shirt. I couldn't look away. There was blood everywhere. Blood had turned B-Budd's white crew cut red. I could see he was crying, and I knew being tied up like that must hurt, and I couldn't help myself—I had to ask. "Mother, why is B-Budd in that awful shirt?"

She shook her head. "It's just the way they do things, Missy, when someone is ranting or going crazy. It calms them down so they go quietly into the paddy wagon." I had no idea what a paddy wagon was, but I guess Mother wasn't thinking, because she stopped the car right near that wagon and she went on talking. She told me the paddy wagon was a padded truck they used to carry people who were out of control away to the hospital. She said "crazy people." That didn't make any sense to me at all. B-Budd was odd, but he wasn't crazy. I started to say that to Mother, but I stopped when I saw those three monster men pushing B-Budd around like he was a garden hose and when I saw Mrs. Hugh standing there holding his pajamas and a pair of brown slide-in slippers and a folded robe up to her chest.

I wondered if B-Budd knew what was going on. Then Mr. Hugh climbed into the wagon with B-Budd, and I felt a little bit better until they shut the doors.

"Mother . . . ," I began, but I wasn't sure what I wanted to ask her, and I wasn't sure Mother knew what to do or say. Luckily, just then Reddaddy came walking toward us. Mother ordered Robertelee and me to stay in the car, and she got out.

I figured I'd better mind her this time. Obviously, something important was going on. I sat very still, and a few minutes later, when she got back in the car, her face was white as her night cream, and Robertelee asked what happened to B-Budd. "Is he crazy?"

Mother talked like she was in a trance. "There's been a horrible accident. . . . What in the world is going to happen now?" She started up the car to get us on home and drove faster than normal. Daddy didn't like anyone to drive fast on the farm, but Mother was speeding and talking about how Daddy was going to be furious. "How could this happen right on our front doorstep? We'll never live it down. That poor little boy never was right."

"Who?" I asked, and I think it must have half-surprised her that anyone was talking to her, because right away she said, "Awful, just awful," and I wanted to know what she meant, but I could see she wasn't going to say anything more.

We reached the garage in record time.

Mother didn't say another word, but she hurried us into the house and told us we had to wait for Reddaddy to come on home, so we just sat there on the front stoop, waiting awhile, until finally Reddaddy and Daddy both came home, and Mother hurried us all into the den.

Reddaddy's face was ghost white, his eyes almost solid red from all the lines crossing them. He gave me a tight hug and said, "Bless you, my granddaughter. I hate that you saw that accident." He turned to Daddy. "Such a terrible accident. What are we going to do, Georgelea? It's an awful scandal."

I must admit, I never knew much about my daddy, like what he thought about most things. He never cried, and when he was mad his face got hard and we all quit talking. All I did know about him came from his chair—The Chair—the one with the ottoman to put his feet up on, the one he had kept since his days at Princeton University, where he graduated with honors. Daddy always sat in that chair, and for a long time my brother and I crawled up into Daddy's lap when he sat there stretched out to read his paperback mysteries or to listen to Gene Autry or Vaughn Monroe or Tommy Dorsey orchestra music. Daddy's lap had been our playground and our refuge, but when we got a little older a bunch of dogs moved in and we moved out, and now Daddy housed up to half a dozen dachshunds that stretched out and around him in that chair and ottoman, and usually Daddy sat there for hours, massaging the ears and feet of his pets as they snored and stretched and pressed on him and growled at each other when one was taking up too much space.

Whenever Daddy was in the house, he was in that chair with his legs propped up on that ottoman—if he'd just come home from the office, he'd be wearing his perfectly polished shoes pointed at the toe with the fine pinholes all over them and tied neatly with thin shoestring. The butler kept his shoes polished. But after tennis Daddy'd be barefoot, his bare toes covered in Mexana powder. He had short toes like me, and the skin on his legs and feet was powder white, like Mother's porcelain china, with blue veins mapped through it. I knew if Daddy had been king, this chair would have been his throne, and I always thought when he was sitting there that he was like God, full of wisdom.

But not that night. That night he was wearing those pointy shoes and his beautiful suit, and he looked sad. His voice was thick with direction when he explained we were all going to just stay calm. "We'll try to help the Hugh family come to terms with their loss," he said. "Mr. Hugh never sent B-Budd or little Bummer to school, and I never saw B-Budd playing with anyone. But he loved that little brother of his."

I still didn't know what was going on, and I wanted to know, so I stepped around those dogs and curled up under Daddy's right arm. Robertelee took the other arm, and Daddy looked at us with his most serious face and said, "It was a careless accident. B-Budd was chopping wood, and he didn't hear Bummer crawl up behind him, 'cause he was yelling out Psalm Twenty-Three . . ."

I knew B-Budd did that. He said it gave rhythm to his chopping.

But this time, Daddy said, Little Bummer sneaked up behind B-Budd like an Indian scout, and when B-Budd reared back with his ax to get in a good swing, that ax landed on Little Bummer's head and split it apart. "The sheriff and the forensic staff thought it best to send B-Budd on up to Boliver, to the mental hospital. He won't go to prison for accidental killing. Not at his age," Daddy told Mother. It was like he'd forgotten we were there.

I studied Daddy's face. I could see he seemed sure about that, even though I couldn't quite take in all the information. Reddaddy looked like he was going to cry or be sick or both, and pretty soon after that he said he'd had enough and was going upstairs to take a nap. No one said anything more that night.

I knew B-Budd was in trouble, and I wanted to help him get better, and I was especially sad because it looked as if the number of playmates I had had been reduced. I had only two I could count in the first place: B-Budd and my cousin, whom Mother forced me to play with, but all she ever wanted to do was play dolls and have tea and crumpets with her doll that looked like Queen Elizabeth, and that didn't seem like fun to me.

I'd never counted my little brother as a playmate, but I thought maybe now I'd have to.

The next day, and every day after that, Mother forbade us to ride our bicycles down to the front of the farm, so every time we passed the front gate going off to school, we looked out the car windows as hard as we could, straining to see what was going on at Mr. Hugh's house. But the doors were closed tight, and shades were drawn on the windows, so we couldn't tell what was happening, except now that spring was halfway over, I noticed the stingers were building nests bigger than ever in the corners of B-Budd's house, and Mr. Hugh had done nothing about it. A couple of rabbit cages had turned over with the rabbits still sitting in them. You'd think Mr. Hugh would have taken care of those rabbits, but he didn't, though he did continue to take care of the Herefords, and I thought maybe he thought of those cows, particularly T-Royal, as son substitutes. He pretty much had his hand on a cow at all hours of the day, and Reddaddy spent a lot of time with him trying to fatten up the Herefords to get them fit for the cow sales.

After that Daddy was more often in a bad mood than a good one. A couple of newspaper men continued to pester him every evening, right as we sat down to dinner, but he just told them they were invading his privacy and hung up. Once, I answered the phone, and a man asked me if I was Mr. Georgelea's little girl and what I thought about the killing.

"I'm a girl. I'm not allowed to think," I said, and I hung up just like Daddy did. When I asked her about it, Mammyrosy said she thought the whole accident was absurd and tragic and that Boliver was an insane asylum about fifty miles down the same highway that went past Bozos. She said they kept the whites and the coloreds separate like they did at public toilets. She knew this because one time her friend went to Boliver after he jumped out a window. She said he was locked up in a cell with white walls and that he used to beat his head against the cell walls day in and day out until he finally killed himself, and every time I thought about that I wanted to cry.

I wanted to visit B-Budd so he'd know I still cared about him, but Mother wouldn't hear of such a thing. When I asked Mammyrosy why Mother said that, "Honey, that hospital don't allow no visitors. They's working on those sick folks' minds and don't want no outside disturbances. It's not like regular hospitals, where they work on bodies."

"You mean Mr. Hugh can't even go?" I asked. That seemed too sad even to think about.

"Not for a while," Mammyrosy said, and I could tell by the way she said it that she was sad about this, too. "It's been awful hard on them Hughs, 'specially since they already lost two sons."

I didn't understand. I knew only about B-Budd and Bummer, but Mammyrosy told me that before I was born, back when Mr. Hugh was working over in Arkansas, he had an older boy who fell off a tractor while he was pulling a hay baler. He got cut up, and his body parts got wrapped up in the bales, and there weren't any doctors out on those farms. Mr. Hugh didn't find out about it until he saw that machine roaming through the pasture without anyone in the driver's seat.

"How horrible," I said, but the truth is, I couldn't imagine what it was like to lose a son or a brother, much less kill one, so I just asked Mammyrosy if I could have some Fig Newtons, and while I was eating them I thought about the time when Robertelee was still in the bassinet and I hit him over the head with my shoe. I was glad I hadn't killed my brother, because as soon as he got older and could play, I realized it wasn't so bad having a brother. I couldn't imagine what B-Budd was thinking in that room with the white walls now that he didn't have a brother anymore—now that he had killed him.

At night I dreamed about frog-gigging. I could see B-Budd, so tall and thin, hurling those spears. I wished I could see him again. I thought if I did, I'd let him save me from sin, if that made him happy.

Five

My grandfather had red hair even on his eightieth birthday, and a lot of people called him Mr. Red, but I always called him Reddaddy. If Mother told Daddy I'd been bad and he had to spank me for it, Reddaddy would hide me in his room or out in the rose garden until Daddy forgot about it. And since Daddy was mostly at work or playing tennis, I always knew if we made it through the dinner hour, I was safe.

It wasn't just his keeping me safe. With Reddaddy, I got to do special things, and most of the time when we did special things, Old Thomas was with us. Reddaddy and Old Thomas were true friends who'd consult each other about a whole lot of things I didn't understand at the time. Every now and then they'd get me out of the big house so I wouldn't get spoiled. That's what Reddaddy said. He said he wanted me to experience the important truths in life. That was important to him. But Reddaddy never joined us at the Lolololo tree. He'd balance himself on the cane he always had with him and say he was just too old for "pasture ventures." Seemed like Frightnin' belonged to both Reddaddy and Old Thomas, and if he wasn't with Reddaddy he was following behind Old Thomas.

My favorite time with Reddaddy was when he took me for a ride on his old bay horse, Seminole. Seminole had once been a champion, but now he was retired and coddled and used for Reddaddy's pleasure rides on Saturday afternoons while Daddy was away playing tennis. As soon as we were out at the barn together, Reddaddy would pull me up in his fancy hand-tooled Western saddle to ride with him around the whole farm while he checked all those white fence lines. He had to make sure no boards were down, no livestock fugitive. He still needed his wooden cane, so when we rode he carried it in a special pouch on his fancy saddle, a pouch made just for it. To me, that cane, shaped like a stick, was the most special thing he had. I always thought it was the kind of cane a Jesus shepherd might have walked with, but from the curved end of Reddaddy's cane you could pull out a long metal bar with numbers he used to measure the height of a particular horse or a cow. Many times when we were out in the back pastures, on the top of a rise, with the sun like a big corn muffin high in the sky, we'd dismount Seminole and stand there studying things. He'd count cows and measure yearlings and scan the land. He'd poke a mound of manure for insects, break off a stalk of seeds to rub through his fingers, kick the dandelions to see if the puffs would fly off, and I'd imitate him.

One day on a Sunday ride while we were standing out there, he looked off into the distant horizon like a soldier spying for Indian war bonnets, and he said, "One day, little lady, all this will be yours. This land. A part of the South."

He turned for a minute and looked at me to make sure I was listening, but when he saw I was paying close attention, he looked out at the horizon again and went on. "You gotta hang onto the land, Missy. When everything else is gone, you still have something of value, a piece of history, a piece of America. It's your identity. They know who you are when you have land. Don't you ever let anyone take it away from you."

I did have one question, though, and it was about Old Thomas. I wondered if he had an identity, too, so I asked Reddaddy if Old Thomas had any land.

He smiled at me. "Old Thomas has all the land, yet it seems he also has none of it," he said. "Old Thomas spent most of his life taking care of your old Reddaddy, so he's lived wherever I've lived.

He never needed to own anything but our secrets, and he's the most loyal man I ever knew. Maybe that's because he comes from the very soil of my birth." Reddaddy began to walk, and I followed him over to a shaky fence. There were six panels in each section of fence, but on this one he pulled at the crossed board and it fell off.

"Weak," he mumbled, and then he went on mumbling and I had to strain to hear him. "Yes, Old Thomas's mother died in having him, and my mother inherited him right off. We suckled from the same breast and grew up picking cotton in the same field, raising hogs for slaughter. We dug the soil where our mothers are buried, right next to the Philadelphia church. It's a hard thing to explain to a young one like you, but you'll know the truth someday."

I was trying hard to understand, but I wasn't sure I did, so I walked over to another section of the fence and pulled on the boards; these didn't move, and Reddaddy seemed glad about that. He called to Seminole, "Come on, old pal, back to the feed trough."

As Reddaddy mounted Seminole, I asked him why I always had to wait to know things. "Maybe everything will be gone by the time I get old enough to know, or you'll forget what you were going to tell me," I said, and I dropped my head in a pout, but Reddaddy pulled me up by one strong arm to sit in the saddle in front of him, tapped Seminole slightly, rubbing his cane gently on the withers where the hair lay backward just to urge him into an easy pace.

"It's tough having to grow up, young'un." He laughed lightly as we rode on, looking for more breaks in the fences, and I knew that was the end of that conversation for that day, so I didn't bother to ask anymore.

A few days later, Reddaddy was in his merciful mood, so he sneaked me out to Bozos, pretending he was going to Sears, Roebuck, which was in truth in the other direction. I think he wanted to get away from the big house because Mother was fussing about Mr. Hugh and B-Budd and why Daddy wouldn't get rid of them, and Reddaddy seemed like he was tired of hearing about all that, so he told Mother we had to go out to Sears, Roebuck to get some things and he wouldn't mind my company.

Sometimes Reddaddy took me into downtown Memphis to the

compress office on Monroe, and sometimes he even took me down to the cotton plant in South Memphis to show me off to the secretaries there. But he especially liked to show me off to Miss Lula and Miss Irma at Bozos, and I preferred Bozos because that's where I got to see Sheriff Ferget, who usually dropped in for a slab of ribs. He had a siren on his squad car because he was the county's most important sheriff, and he swirled the red light when he arrived, just so we'd know.

I liked the Bozos sisters. Miss Irma was tough as our old mules, but she was an expert on clouds and the sizes of raindrops and she told lots of stories. She was always talking about the weather, like a radio that never turned off, and Reddaddy said she was a good forecaster and that it helped the hunters to know how the weather was behaving when they were getting ready to set out. The hunters usually came to Bozos to eat before they went off scouting quail or deer. Even Sheriff Ferget sort of relied on Miss Irma as a human barometer.

Miss Lula was quieter than Miss Irma. She watched herself. You could see her back in the back through the open window behind the takeout counter, where the barbecue pit was. I think she liked being back there, where she got her business done and didn't have to talk so much. Miss Lula did secret cookings—like her lemon meringue pie with meringue icing that was, she said, a mile high. She didn't sell it, but she did give it to her favorite customers. If Reddaddy and Sheriff Ferget were talking too long about dogs and hunting trips, she'd cut the pie and bring them a piece so they'd get distracted and forget what they were talking about and change the subject. Lots of people said the two sisters reminded them of Martha and Mary from the time of Jesus, but I wasn't sure I understood that. I just knew I liked them.

I wasn't supposed to be at Bozos, but Reddaddy would just about have climbed a big oak if he'd thought it would make me happy. He was well aware of the fact that I was short on friends I liked to play with, so he often made up an excuse to take me away from the big house, and whenever he took me to Bozos I had to be extra careful not to spill sauce on my blouse, or else Mother would find out where

I'd been. Usually Miss Irma wrapped me in a bib before she brought me some ribs. "Come on in, y'all," she would shout when the screen door creaked open. When Sheriff Ferget arrived, he usually had a new joke for Miss Irma and a bag of baby tomatoes, homegrown down at the station. Sheriff Ferget told awful jokes, but they always made Miss Irma fold down at the waist with laughter.

"I feel a tornado coming on today," she mentioned, after we sat down. "Them radio men never get those warnings right. By the time we're told something's coming, it's here, already done its damage and gone on. Ferget, remember that time you had to hole up in an outhouse?" Miss Irma was up to mischief—even I could see that.

"Now, Miss Irma, enough of that," the sheriff said, trying to bat the story away, but she was ahead of him. "That tornado hit like a boot on a bug, and when the ol' shack rose up, there you was, reading the Sears catalog and relieving yourself. Only thing that kept you from flying off with it was your belt loop got stuck between the wood cracks of the seat. How the Lord does save." She went off smiling so hard it hurt.

Bozos was always full of people eating slabs of ribs dripping with the sisters' vinegary sauce. The tables were covered with red-checked cloths that were plasticized so a mess could be wiped up quicker. We sat in chairs that had a bit of spring in the back if you leaned back too hard. At both ends of the dining room were big windows to see what was going on in the distant ravines and pine forests, and sometimes when I looked out I'd see a deer standing there in a pose. Inside on the walls there were pictures of Coca-Cola girls in shorts, a stuffed duck, a rack of deer horns, some brown photographs of hogs with big ribbons on their ears, and a plaster cross, colored red and white, saying JESUS SAVES.

Sheriff Ferget walked around shaking hands. A lot of folks were asking him about the Hugh killing. That day I was there, he got some help with the answers because the county judge had brought his wife in for lunch. She mostly smiled and kept her napkin up close to her mouth to wipe off the sauce drool, but the judge listened to people's questions—what happened to Mr. Hugh's kid, and what was the meaning of it all?

The judge thought it was a sad story, but he called it "a cut-and-dried case of an accident."

"I heard the boy was lost in some sort of religious trance, being one of those Holy Rollers," Miss Irma said.

"As loud as he was shouting, he wouldn't have heard an elephant stampede. It was a freak accident," the judge continued.

"B-Budd is my playmate," I interrupted. "I wish he would come home and . . ." But Reddaddy gave me a hushing sign, so I stopped talking.

The judge wiped barbecue sauce off his fingers. "I'm worried about that boy and whether his family can handle him," he said, but Reddaddy told him, "Mr. Hugh's the best cattleman I've ever been around. He's made T-Royal into a champion sire."

"The Hughs are faithful churchgoers," Sheriff Ferget inserted. "Belong to the Dolly Pond Church of God with Signs Following. That religion has some strange ideas."

"Heard their pastors have been dying from snakebites," Miss Irma added. "They was kissing poisonous snakes in the mouth and sticking their fingers into electric outlets to see if they'd live to tell about it." She shook her head. "I'd choose a safer religion."

The sheriff shook his head, too. "Yep," he said. "They don't cotton to no doctors, either. It was the bloodiest site I have ever been called to. I still can't get it out of my head. What with Mrs. Hugh weeping and wailing and throwing eggs and dead pigeons at B-Budd . . . quite a mess to clean up before it was over with. But what was hell was fitting that little brother back together. We had to wrap him in a tow sack before the medics could get him into the ambulance."

By then I could see everyone had forgotten about me and the judge's wife, who was so quiet you could hear her eyes blink. Then Reddaddy noticed I was hearing too much, and he leaned over and said, "Little Missy, why don't you go back and help Miss Lula wash dishes? I bet she's getting lonely back there with only Frightnin' to keep her company."

I liked helping Miss Lula. She asked me to test her sauces and gave me jobs pulling the tender pork off juicy pig legs. Sometimes she told me secrets. She didn't have to tell me about beechos. I already knew about them, except I'd never tasted them.

"Can I try some beechos, Miss Lula?" I was collecting leftovers in paper sacks to throw in the garbage cans. Frightnin' was watching every move I made—though by then I'd have thought he'd be stuffed.

"Honey child, I'm afraid of what they might do to you. . . . Old Thomas is real cautious about when beechos are right."

"I don't think they'd bother me, Miss Lula."

"True, dear—Old Thomas told me you's acquainted with beechos—but I'se wary on them effects." She turned and went out the swinging door that always hit a B flat when it swung back and forth. I waited for her, figuring out my arguments, and when she came back in she had a load of dirty plates up her arms. "Miss Lula," I said, "I help Old Thomas when he collects beechos and dog wafers. Now I'm working on a plan and I need some ideas."

"What's a youngster like you doing working on a plan? You young'uns sure grow up fast."

I leaned close to whisper. "Miss Lula, I don't mind telling you. But it's a big, secret plan. You can't tell a soul."

"Not a soul," she echoed.

"I've got to help B-Budd. He's in some serious trouble."

"Bless his soul." Miss Lula bowed her head.

"Old Thomas says beechos are best at religious curing, though I've never really known something beechos cured. But I know Old Thomas brings them to you for your recipe, and your recipe can make a Siamese cat turn into a Persian one. . . . Well, that's what happened at the Lolololo tree when a cat got hold of some dropped beechos."

"There's more to it than that, Missy," Miss Lula said quietly. "I just don't want to cause no stir. I wish Old Thomas was here so's I could be sure."

"Why don't you call him on the telephone?" I said. I sensed I was maybe getting closer to those beechos.

But Miss Lulu shook her head. "Oh, no, no, I ain't disturbin' Old Thomas on his day off. Well, let me see what I can find." She turned around twice in the center of the kitchen, touched her nose twice, and then closed her eyes a few seconds and started making a strange sound like she was whistling through a flute. Out of nowhere, a tiny flowered purple sack appeared in her hands. It smelled of gingerbread like Mammyrosy made at Christmas, and for a moment, it sucked all the tomato and vinegar odors out of the kitchen. Miss Lula moved to the barbecue pit, reached her thin white hand into the oven, and took hold of something inside that made her arm shine like polished silver and set off stripes of light like sparklers. She slid out a tiny jar with a cross on its side. Well, I guess it was a jar. It was as brown as the bricks. She tapped some of the beechos out of the bag and into the jar and stirred it up with her forefinger, but when she took out her finger, it was clean as if she had run it under clear water.

Then Miss Lula walked over to where I was pulling pork, and with two long, thin fingers, she picked up one of those blackened crunchy pieces that I liked best and said, "Now dab it," so I took the piece and dabbed it into the jar. The pork piece just flat disappeared, either melted or dissolved, I don't know.

"Drink from the jar lip," she said quietly.

I did, and handed the jar back to her. And then I could feel it all in me. It was better than anything I'd ever had felt. It eased through me like melted marshmallows, tasted like chocolate and peanuts at one moment, then asparagus with Hollandaise, then cream of tomato soup. As soon as one taste went by, another came up. It wasn't sweet, but it made my lips red like Reddaddy's hair.

Then suddenly Miss Lula shrank smaller, or I got taller, one or the other, and I realized I was lifting up. I lifted up and twirled and twisted and tumble-saulted and swam and flapped my arms like eagle wings. Then I just stretched out and crossed my legs like I was lying in my bed. I could do all kinds of things acrobatic and I could go where I wanted to just by thinking it.

Miss Lula didn't even look. She had gone over to the counter window to make sure no one was aiming his eyes in the direction of the kitchen.

"Can you see me, Miss Lula?" I asked.

She said nothing, but I knew Frightnin' could see me. He was sitting straight up now, his tongue hanging out, his eyes on me and his ears lifted as much as a hound dog can lift up his ears.

"Look, Miss Lula!" Tiny red hearts began shooting out of my knee, the one with the three rocks in it. *Pow, pow, pow.* They moved all around me and tickled, and as I looked down, I saw the kitchen was surrounded by thick green stalks with bumpy tops—giant broccoli stalks, big as forests, making a big circle around the room, keeping out anyone who might come in. I sat on top of one of the bunches and thought I was in the Emerald City, beautiful and green, my favorite color.

Miss Lula was probably wondering how long this would last, so she busied herself opening Dr. Pepper bottles and placing them on a tray while Frightnin' began to whine as if he didn't like me up so high and might be going to say something.

Of course, I wasn't going anywhere.

Miss Lula was mumbling. "Those beechos do it every time. You've got to keep pennies in your shoes and your hands on the counter. Old Thomas tells me this every time we do some experimenting. Hands on the counter, he says. Bones in the pockets. Pennies in the shoes. Oh dear. I wasn't thinking. Come on down, young'un, before we gets discovered. You've had one too many beechos. And I can't go out that door till things are back to normal."

So I twisted one last time and caught some of the red hearts and put them in my sweater pocket, and I landed right alongside Frightnin', who paid no attention anymore. It was over. Miss Lula went out the swinging door with the B flat and served the Dr. Peppers, and I decided I'd best go back to pulling pork. I took a nibble or two when no one was looking, but now I knew I had to get hold of some of those beechos. Now I was sure I could do something for B-Budd.

Six

Problems arose every day at B-Budd's house. For one thing, his rabbits kept on multiplying so fast, without B-Budd there to count them, that Reddaddy had to tell Mr. Hugh to trim them down before they took over the farm. As it was, they began to disappear and Mr. Hugh got stirred up and started rooting up trouble for Old Thomas. He accused him of stealing B-Budd's rabbits and roasting them for supper.

My brother and I rode slow as snails on our bikes, following Old Thomas and a bunch of unknown hound dogs on the way down to his house. He had eaten chitlins for lunch and had a handful he was offering to his sniffing companions along the way. A dirty red truck pulled up the driveway fast and spun in a circle, making a ring of dust. When it settled, there was Sheriff Ferget right beside the truck in his police car, the red lights flashing.

"Trouble's a-brewing, mm-hmm," mumbled Old Thomas. We got off our bikes and walked closer to Old Thomas's house.

"Hi, Sheriff. Can I see your gun?" my brother cried, racing his bicycle up to Sheriff Ferget's side.

Sheriff Ferget patted Robertelee on the head. "Not today, cowboy—we got some things to do," and, readjusting his belt with the holster and handcuffs hanging on it, he said, "Old Thomas, I don't like these kids being here, but we gotta talk."

Two really fat men wearing International Harvester hats slid out of the seat in the dirty truck. Drawn on their arms and faces were scary monsters and snakes chewing on something they kept trying to spit out through holes in their teeth. Those men smelled worse than onions.

Mr. Hugh came and stood by Sheriff Ferget like they were buddies.

"Old Thomas, I gotta run you in," the sheriff said. "You've been accused of stealing rabbits. Come on down to the station with me so we can get to the bottom of this."

I was frozen to my bicycle.

Old Thomas didn't say a word, not even when Mr. Hugh and his ugly friends called him nasty names as he was loading up in the sheriff's car.

"Handcuff that nigger," one of the uglies cried out.

"I ain't gonna handcuff anyone, you bugger. Shut up, or I'll run you in, too," the sheriff said firmly. "You kids go on home, you hear?"

Old Thomas got to sit in the front seat of the sheriff's squad car. Both the fat men spit on the ground and banged the metal doors of their pickup truck extra loud when they pushed themselves back into it.

The sheriff didn't leave right off. I could see Old Thomas through the half-shut window. He nodded his head and started getting back out of the car.

"What's going on, Ferget?" one of the ugly men shouted. They climbed back out of the truck, but Sheriff Ferget seemed happier, and he turned to Old Thomas and said, "Lead us on," and Old Thomas and all the rest of us—dogs, too—began parading in the direction of his back porch, and all the while Old Thomas talked.

"Mr. Sheriff," he said, "every morning when I pass on to the out-house, I sees a whole crop of new rabbits resting under my front porch. Figured they was producing and liked the quietness under there, away from the dogs. I knowed they was snitching all the let-tuce in my garden, but dey's hungry. I suspected they came from Master B-Budd's collection. Dey's fine-looking. Seeing he was receiving treatment up at Boliver hospital, I suspected dey's lonely.

No matter dem eating my garden. Plain forgot to mention it to Mr. Hugh, but I notified Mr. Red that he may not get no fresh lettuce for a while."

And then, sure enough, we all saw it: a bunch of strange-colored rabbits enjoying the overflow of Old Thomas's garden. For a minute the rabbits looked up and hopped once or twice, then went back to chewing up Reddaddy's favorite Bibb lettuce.

"Mr. Hugh, why didn't you just ask Old Thomas before causing all this disturbance?" Sheriff Ferget asked. "I ain't got time to waste."

Old Thomas laid his hand on the lifted-up back porch and leaned close to Robertelee and me so we'd be the only ones to hear. "I don't think these rabbits is hankering to be kilt," he said, and we didn't say anything, but we watched Sheriff Ferget getting back in his car.

"Well, what's your verdict now?" he said to Mr. Hugh.

"Leave the damn rabbits in Old Thomas's garden," Mr. Hugh whined. "I ain't got no time for B-Budd's rabbits. I've got to get Mr. Red's cattle ready and haul my wife over to Boliver every time they open the door. B-Budd ain't gonna know a rabbit from a stinger in the state he's in."

"Mr. Hugh, how's your boy coming along?" Sheriff Ferget asked kindly.

I listened closely, because that was what I wanted to know, too.

"I can't rightly say today." Mr. Hugh scrunched up his face as he stepped up on the sideboard of that truck. Right at the face of the fat men, he said quietly, so maybe we couldn't hear him as we rode off, though we heard loud and clear, "That dag-blasted nigger gets out of every fix he gets into."

"Just you wait," said the driver, whose stomach was so large the steering wheel couldn't move unless he inhaled. "We'll get him." But secretly I bet Mr. Hugh was wrong about B-Budd. He'd still know those rabbits by name. He loved those rabbits.

I wished I could see B-Budd again, even though he liked to say I was a spoiled rich kid. I didn't know what he meant by that, except that maybe my house was bigger than his, but every time he said it, it made me mad. Besides, I didn't like having to go to the rich girls' school and talk about the things the rich girls in my class talked about. I was in third grade that year, 1948, and those girls knew nothing about snakes and frogs and secret things, and naturally I could never lift up around them because anytime they didn't like what I said or did, they'd run and tell the teacher, and I couldn't risk anyone's knowing about the beechos and lifting up.

I liked playing with B-Budd lots more than I liked being around those girls, the ones everyone liked most, who had charm bracelets with so many charms there wasn't room to hang anymore. Those girls spent most of their time at the swimming pool at the Memphis Country Club. Like the other spoiled rich kids, I spent an awful lot of that hot summer at that swimming pool, but I didn't want to. It didn't even have a fairgrounds with a Zippin Pippin and a Ferris wheel, like the public pool did. I told Mother that was where I wanted to go, but she said nice people didn't go there. "You get diseases there," she said. She said it was because everyone peed in the pool water.

I used to wonder if there were any pools for colored people. At the country club colored waiters in white jackets served Cokes and I thought maybe they didn't like to swim. I didn't know, but I didn't ask. I wasn't supposed to ask.

That summer when B-Budd was gone, Mother drove Robertelee and me to town to the club almost every day so she could play golf or tennis. I'd hide out in the women's locker room, which smelled like wet socks, as long as I could. I didn't want to sit poolside, where I'd have to be nice to girls I didn't like. All I thought about was whether those people in their bathing suits and bathing caps knew what had happened on our farm, and if they did what they thought about that.

There was another problem at the pool. I was embarrassed to wear my bathing suit because it exposed my chubby, freckled skin, and I could see people looking. And also I wasn't fast enough to win swimming races. Mostly when we were there I spent time alone. No one wanted to do cartwheels and handstands with me underwater, but underwater was the only place to hide, and most days my nose was stopped up after all that twisting and twirling and trying to look graceful underwater, where I was practicing to be Esther Williams rising up out of the water in a pose.

Since Mother said I had to be prepared to be a proper girl, every fall she sent me to Miss Hutchinson's School for Girls, and Robertelee went to kindergarten at a private boys' school. Miss Hutchinson's was an hour away, in Memphis. It was at that school I learned the word "hate," because the girls there were always saying things like, "I hate doing this or that," or "I hate how so-and-so wears her hair," or "I hate that dress," and I could tell most of those girls hated me. Every day all I waited for was three o'clock, when Old Thomas picked me up. Then we'd pick up Robertelee, and while we drove back to the farm, Old Thomas would tell us trick jokes. Usually we could talk him into stopping at Hopper's General Store to get some Clark bars and root beer, even when Mother had told him not to.

In fourth grade, when my classmates learned my daddy had a horse farm, their attitudes began to change. Instead of hating me, they envied me, and they wanted to spend the day with me riding horses. I became more popular, but I didn't care, and I didn't want anybody to come spend the day at the farm. I just let them think they would be invited one of these days, but I didn't invite them, and I didn't tell Mother they wanted to come. If I told her, she'd want me to invite those girls to our house. But I knew they weren't really my friends.

Mother got our mind off things we didn't like by taking us to the Ringling Brothers Circus, which came to town every spring. I don't think she liked the smell of the elephants and tigers, and she didn't let us stop to see the freak show. We had to go straight to the big top without even stopping to buy pink cotton candy or Cracker Jacks. "You'll get sick to your stomach eating that junk," she said. But one year, even though she was reluctant, she bought me a chameleon on a chain that one of the clowns was selling. It did little miracles, like changing colors depending on what color it sat on. I couldn't wait to get home to show Old Thomas, because Old Thomas was the one I showed everything miraculous to. He was the one I confided in more than anyone.

Seven

The day after we went to the circus, Robertelee and I were sitting on the front steps of the portico side of the house, looking lost because there were no more colors to test my chameleon with. He was pinned to my pink sweater to rest. I could smell the perfume of the magnolias on the big trees lining the back pasture. The azaleas planted against every wall of the house were a variety of reds and pinks. I was paying attention to all those smells and colors when Old Thomas waved to us to come with him to the back pasture. Frightnin' was alongside him, snapping at the bees. "Come on, young'uns," he called, and I was overjoyed that we could go to the Lolololo tree. Even Robertelee jumped up and down three times and started running.

"Hold on there, Mister Robertelee," Old Thomas said. "We'll get there jest as easy in a walk as in a run." Then he looked over at my sweater. "What's that you got on there, Missy?" he asked.

"It's Herbert, my chameleon. Mother bought it for me at the circus."

"Lordy, Missy, hope I don't have to resurrect this poor little thing like I did your pink turtle." That's what Mother had bought me at the circus the year before.

"It's magic, Old Thomas. The clown said Herbert would be the color of whatever color I wear."

Old Thomas laughed and fixed his hat securely on his head, denting it well in the middle.

We were walking through the high grasses. The birds and the bees were traveling with us, and that reminded me of a question I wanted to ask. "What do they mean by 'the birds and the bees'?"

Old Thomas shook his head, disturbing one of the airmail birds trying to settle there. "Lordy, Missy, that day'll come."

"What day?" I asked.

"The one when you's gonna know all about the birds and the bees." I could tell by the way he turned his head he wasn't going to say anymore, but I always believed Old Thomas when he said one day I'd know.

Must have been half a dozen dogs of little description resting along our secret path, each one with a strange case of hair curls. Each one sat up to attention when we passed, like they were waiting for a word from their general. As we went by, they lay back down. A whole group of green snakes pressed down the path of grass for us so we wouldn't get tangled up in it. Airmail birds swooped in figure eights and dropped pink petals from their mouths into my hair. The population of all these creatures had expanded, and the moment we came in view of the tree, my dress began flashing colors like a rainbow that couldn't make up its mind. Neon colors. Flower-petal colors. Crayon colors.

Herbert was so confused, not knowing what color to be, that I thought it best to unpin him and hold him in my hand, and my dress went back to pink. So I decided to untie the string and place Herbert on the white bark of the Lolololo. I thought he'd be safer there, but when I let him go free, the tree began to flash the same array of colors as my dress, and white birds, appearing out of nowhere, dipped and soared with whirligigs in their beaks. Old Thomas smiled and said not a word. He only hummed, and Herbert the chameleon disappeared.

"Where'd he go, Old Thomas?" I asked.

"Might have gone to visit his family," Old Thomas replied. "I gave him permission." He didn't have much tolerance for animals people sold as trinkets in the circus, so it didn't surprise me he'd given Herbert permission to leave, and once he was gone, I turned my attention to what was on my mind, what I'd been wanting to ask Old Thomas for a long time now.

"Why can't we send some airmail birds over to fix up B-Budd?" I asked.

He looked at me real hard and thought a little while. "Ain't so easy, Missy. Ain't so easy." He shook his head. "Master Hugh ain't ready for that kind of intervention. I knows they loves Jesus, but they ain't got it right yet. They don't let no one inside them that don't line up straight with their own thinking. No, Missy, it just ain't a fruitful time."

I knew he must be right, and even though I didn't like it, I accepted it the way I accepted everything Old Thomas told me. We settled on our favorite stumps, and I noticed the beechos had grown long stems. Old Thomas rubbed them off into a hankie, and ladybugs flew away. A moment later, when Old Thomas finished his cleaning, they flew back to the trunk. There were so many birds' nests on the branches, the Lolololo tree looked like it was wearing a chirping, squeaking wig. Between the thick roots that reached out into the pasture a pretty good distance to accommodate extra O-holes for needy snakes, there were clumps of green, like miniature forests. I looked at them, and I looked at Old Thomas. "Look at those baby forests," I said, but he didn't turn around. He knew what I was talking about.

"Yes'm, Missy, them's broccoli forests. I scattered some seeds out there in the winter, and they's fruitifying."

"I don't like broccoli at all, Old Thomas. It stinks when Mammyrosy cooks it."

I could see him smile even though he still hadn't turned around. I thought he must have some sort of secret he just wasn't going to let me know. Then he was humming and looking out on the world through his white eye, and for the first time in a long time, I felt good, being there with Old Thomas, seeing some magic stuff, listening to the animal chatter. I wondered if God was around, if God was like the wind, which you can't see but can feel.

I wished the day would never end.

Of course then it did, and we had to go back to the big house for dinner.

Eight

One afternoon that summer, Reddaddy took his weekly trip with Old Thomas down to the plant in South Memphis, and they let me come along. That helped me stop thinking about B-Budd. I loved standing by those huge compress machines, so big they went through the roof of the building. I watched the colored men slipping in and out of the centers as they strapped the bales tighter and tighter. I knew it was a dangerous job and that someone might lose a hand or a leg or his whole self—I knew because Daddy said so. The balers yelled off numbers in a strange slang, and then they jumped out of the way just as the machine steamed down again, squeezing the cotton bale smaller and smaller. I liked the rhythm and quickness about their movements. I felt as if I were watching a tribal dance.

Reddaddy had a heart for every kind of compress activity because he was one of the inventors, and he spent hours watching those cotton bales pop out of the compress smaller than when they went in, cinched tight with metal strips. He said he could relax best when he was talking cotton gossip with the balers, especially when Old Thomas was along. Old Thomas checked up on the recruits he had trained when he was down there—that was before he moved up to the farm. It had been a while since Reddaddy and Old Thomas officially retired from the plant, and they both said they could never stay away for long.

When it got late in the day, the men invited us to join the late shift for their supper—chicken-fried steak accompanied by a pile of mashed potatoes and gravy, cooked right in the plant cafeteria. Big John was the head cook, the same Big John who cooked at the compress picnics at the farm. Even I knew that chicken-fried steak was terrible for Reddaddy's heart. I knew that because Mother said it was so, but when I asked him if he thought he ought to eat it, he just said, "No need of living if I can't enjoy the fruits of Big John's labor now and then." And I had to agree it tasted especially good. At home we were never allowed to eat fried things.

When Old Thomas went up to the counter for another helping, a strange baldheaded man jumped up and started to yell, "You nigger! You upstart! You ain't got no right to a second helpin' before I go up there!" and when he did that the whole room fell silent as air through a dandelion, but the man kept on yelling. "Who knows what poisons he's passing on that serving spoon? I don't want no crazy nigger filling my potatoes with something I don't know." He threw his tray on the floor, and then he reached over and threw Old Thomas's tray, too. Then he marched right out the cafeteria door, and Reddaddy stood up and went over and put his hand on Old Thomas's shoulder. He began to apologize for the man's rude behavior, and then he said he was going to find out from Superintendent Doggit who that man was.

Even from across the room, I could hear the words coming out of Reddaddy's mouth. He was madder than I had ever seen him. "I won't have anybody with that kind of philosophy working in my plant," he said, looking at all those people sitting there with their mouths hanging open. "Ladies and gentlemen, we ain't got no room for that kind of behavior in this plant. We are all equal, and we eat with whom we want when we want."

I looked around and saw heads nodding, and I heard the men starting to mumble in agreement, and I was glad about that, but I knew my face was red, so I kept my head down. It was hard to look Old Thomas in the eye, so I looked down and ate my mashed potatoes. But pretty soon he came over and patted me on the head and excused himself and went out into the plant to get some tools he needed to borrow for work at the farm, and Reddaddy went off to talk to Mr. Doggit, so I just finished eating my food.

When Reddaddy came out of the office, it was already dark outside, and he said it was time to go. I hadn't eaten my cherry cobbler yet, and I wanted to, but he said if he didn't get me home soon, Daddy would accuse him of spoiling me, and then he said good-bye to everyone, even Big John back in the kitchen. We walked to the large metal shipping entrance through a part of the plant where the cotton bales were stacked five high and six deep, and outside Reddaddy put me in the seat of the pickup truck and said for me to stay quiet.

"We gotta wait for Old Thomas," he said. "I better go see if I can help him." He picked up an armful of tow sacks and tossed them in the pickup—he liked to use them to load up feed for the daily rounds to the cow and horse pastures. And the next thing I knew, we were driving home on those dark roads, and I knew I'd fallen asleep. Sheriff Ferget's squad car was leading us, and when we reached the big house, I noticed Reddaddy was having trouble balancing on his cane.

"You all right, Mr. Red?" Sheriff Ferget asked, holding Reddaddy's arm as he climbed up the front stairs. At the door Daddy took over, and after the sheriff checked Reddaddy good, he got back in his car to answer his beeping walkie-talkie. He took off with the red light whirling.

"I've done exerted myself more than these ol' bones can take," Reddaddy mumbled to Daddy. I noticed he had white bird feathers in his hair and cotton all over his seersucker pants, and he walked directly up the stairs to his room without hugging me good night, so even I was a little bit worried about him, and I wondered if it was the food or if it was that man who'd said those terrible things that had taken so much out of Reddaddy.

But then I spied dessert on the dining room table and I asked Mother if I could have some. "Please," I begged, because it was meringue covered in custard, one of my favorites. Usually I wasn't allowed even a bite of dessert at dinnertime, because Mother didn't want me to be fat, but tonight she said, "Oh, maybe a little," and I ate some and she sent me off to bed. I didn't fall asleep right away. I was thinking about what was wrong with Old Thomas eating chicken-fried steak with us and about what had worn out Reddaddy so much he hadn't even hugged me good night.

Nine

A few weeks later, Reddaddy took me to Bozos and Sheriff Ferget
arrived at the same time we did. We had hardly gotten in the
screen door when Miss Irma, all in a dither, jumped at the sheriff
with loud words about some customers who had just left.

"Sons of dogs, they were. Sons of the worst dogs. Sheriff, there's
some trouble stirring up in this county." I moved in close to hear
everything they said, because I had a feeling this had something
to do with what had happened to Old Thomas at the plant. Sheriff
Ferget told Miss Irma to calm down two degrees, but Miss Irma
could barely restrain herself, and she said to Reddaddy, "You
better hear this, too, Mr. Red." Whatever it was that was working
her up was something I wanted to hear, but Reddaddy remembered I was there, and he told me to get out to the kitchen. "Miss
Lula is full of work for you," he said. I knew it was pointless to
protest.

Miss Lula was carting in wood from out back, letting the screen
door slam every single time. She had to let out a big heave to lift
up those big pieces of wood, so I hurried outside to the wood pile,
which was right under the window with the big view, so I could
help—and so I heard the words coming out of the window. Miss
Irma was talking so loud even the fish in a nearby pond could hear

her. When I peeked inside, I could see the customers standing in a circle around her waiting to hear. So I waited, too.

"Listen, two redneck types wearing filthy boots showed up here jest an hour ago. They'd been tromping through something worse than mud. I ain't gonna describe their odor. Seems like one of them been messing around in your back pasture, Mr. Red. They said they was hunting rabbits. Now, I ask ya, how did he get into the back pasture, and for what? Rabbits?"

The sheriff moved in close, and I watched him try to get a bit of order going, because Miss Irma's hair was all mixed up from her pulling at it, and she was talking so fast it was hard for him to understand. It was hard for anyone.

"Two of them fellows stomped in here and stood with them tattooed arms crossed over their chests, looking around, and finally they sat down and ordered coffee and that made me suspicious. Why'd anyone come to Bozos to order coffee? Coffee's awful here. Why didn't they order barbecue?"

Even though the sheriff was trying to get a word in edgewise, Miss Irma wasn't finished.

"They talked about some fella named Jerry who stumbled into your back pasture, Mr. Red. When he crawled out of a gully, a whole collection of snakes with red bandages wrapped around their bodies attacked him, and their pal was as frightened as a bloodsucker on a leather boot. Took off in the other direction with piss running down his leg. Dropped his shotgun in a pile of horse manure."

I could see Sheriff Ferget wanted to laugh. I kind of wanted to laugh, too, but I wasn't supposed to be hearing this, so I held my breath. I think that's what the sheriff must have done, too.

"When he went back for his gun, he found it poking up half out of some snake hole and he couldn't get it out. Been packed in with horse, cow, and chicken manure dried into something harder than bricks, and bird feathers were sticking out like an Indian headdress, and even when he wrestled he couldn't get nothing to budge. Shotgun was a loaner. That's what they said," and that last part did it—Sheriff Ferget couldn't hold back his laughter. But that only egged Miss Irma on.

"The one called Buddy was madder than skunk spray. Said he figured it was the fella with the white eye causing all the trouble, 'cause he was a voodoo doctor. And they were going to look stupid in front of some Imperial Wizard when they showed up without the shotgun."

Now Sheriff Ferget started pacing. I guessed he was figuring out what to do. Miss Irma's eyes were following him like magnets. She said she was upset because she didn't know what the Wizard's folks were doing in these parts and why they were concerned with Old Thomas.

"I heard some talk," the sheriff said. "Stirrer uppers. That's all they are for now, Miss Irma."

When the sheriff looked up, I quickly bent down and picked up three blocks of firewood so they wouldn't know I was listening, but after that I couldn't stop thinking about Old Thomas, and the very next day I went to find him in the barn. I told him I had to go look for something out at the Lolololo tree. "Got some time?" I asked.

"Now what's done stirred you up, Missy?" he asked. "What's you gotta find?"

"Just something I heard," I said. I wasn't even sure what else to say, and I knew he'd take me to the tree. He never said no.

So that very afternoon we moved out of the high weeds into a dusty path, and as we were nearing the Lolololo tree, a group of green snakes welcomed us with lovely S-curves. They flattened out the grasses so the dust wasn't stirred up, and Old Thomas saluted each visitor by name before he eased into humming and singing one of his favorites, the one about chariots taking him home.

Frightnin' was ahead of us, and he began to bark and run forward, but his companions loped along after him with noses to the ground. As we caught up with the hounds, Old Thomas began shouting and waving his hat in his hand: "Y'all no-goods get out of here." Airmail doves flew in designs far up in the sky.

I squinted to see who he was waving at, and I saw, scampering away, their legs tangling up in the tall grass, a couple of white boys with crew cuts like B-Budd's. They were waving slingshots and tossing rocks over their shoulders as they scattered in all directions, leap-frogging logs and chanting, "Voodoo, voodoo. We're gonna get that old nigger. Voodoo." We heard them yelping and screaming as they tried to jump the white board fences Daddy had rigged with electrical wire to keep out trespassers.

"Voodoo, hoodoo, ooh-wee." Old Thomas shook his head in disgust. Sweat beaded on his face, but he didn't wipe it off. He checked to see that his gallon jar of dog wafers was still hidden in the hollowed trunk. They were still there, and he looked mightily relieved. For a while I just watched him calming down, but I couldn't help myself. I had to ask him what voodoo was.

He looked over at me. "It's devil trickery, which he uses to snatch up no-count people," he said. "Voodoo come over on dem slave ships back in the first times. My 'cestors toted with dem special spirits."

"Why?" I asked. I wasn't sure I understood.

"'Cestors didn't know about Jesus, Missy. When they did, they was happy to take up with Him, but a few didn't want to forget voodoo."

"Is voodoo good or bad, Old Thomas?" I asked.

He smiled. "There's bad and good in all traditions. Somes is protected, and somes is not. It depends on yo heart, Missy. Depends on yo heart."

I suppose I must have looked a little afraid then, because those boys had rattled my nerves talking about this voodoo stuff. But Old Thomas smiled at me, and his voice had that sound of reassurance he sometimes used with me. "It's best you don't think about those things. The devil ain't studdin' your soul no how. Your heart's genuine good. As long as someone's praying you up, Jesus protects you with His armor. Voodoo can't pull no tricks through that."

I looked around. I had had this question stuck in my mind ever since I'd overheard Miss Irma talking about those men and Old Thomas, so I asked him. I had to ask him. "Old Thomas, can voodoo cause something to get stuck where it can't get out?"

For a while he barely moved, but then he began to slowly nod. "Well now, Missy," he said, "voodoo magic depends on who's running it."

I looked around some more, thinking about the scene Miss Irma had described. I still didn't see any shotguns sticking up out of the ground, at least nowhere near the Lolololo tree. "What's a soul, then, Old Thomas?" These questions had been dogging me, and now that I had Old Thomas's attention and we were in the most sacred spot, I knew I could ask. He had walked over to the tree and was caressing the branch that had the most dog leaves. It bent down of its own volition, and he picked off a few of the ripest ones, and then he said, real slowly, "Ooh-wee, Missy, your askins would keep an honest preacher nervous."

"I just want to know," I said softly.

"A soul is what you got that no one else got," he said, still picking off those dog leaves and not looking at me. "What you do with your soul is how things turn out." Finally he turned and looked at me again, and I knew he could read the question I had in my mind. I needed to know what kind of soul I had.

"You's got good soul, Missy, good soul," he said. "Now, when you gets grown-up and are accumulatin' wisdom, you may get tore up by temptation to do no-good things that sound good. If you fall into temptation, you can still plug back into the eternal light of Jesus by apologizin'. When it's time to go up yonder, a soul should have light bright enough that God won't miss it when He is searching for His saints."

I was listening hard, but the thought that I might fall into temptation gave me a little fright. As far as I knew, there wasn't any light turned on inside me, and I worried about that. "How come everyone says the Jesus people get souls and lights and armor and things and I never get any?" I asked.

"In time, young'un, in time. You got these things already, but you jest ain't awares. Like I keep shining up your daddy's shoes every day so they give him long service, you got to keep shining up your Jesus thinking jest to let Him know you are considering Him."

And even though I had more questions and I wasn't sure of anything, that's when Old Thomas faded off into humming, closing his eyes, his chest expanding and contracting strongly. He began to chant, "Got God's shield, got God's armor suit, got God's helmet, even my shoes. Devil ain't holding on me."

And that very night I had a dream.

I think it was a dream. At least, something caused me to wake up. Maybe it was the *clickety-clank, clickety-clank* I heard coming closer and closer to my window. I wondered if it was the bogey-man or if someone was working voodoo, but I didn't really want to know. I certainly didn't want to look, but I heard a *tap tap tap* on the window, and someone called my name through the metal Venetian blinds. When I peeked, there stood Old Thomas, dressed in a white outfit like Prince Valiant in melted marshmallow. On his chest he had a fuchsia heart cut out like a messy valentine. He juggled three tiny pebbles, or maybe they were chocolate kisses, and he said, "Look at me, Missy. Now I've got on the armor of God. Can you see?"

I laughed at him through my sleepy eyes. "You look like a biscuit," I said.

"Let me show you how it works." Old Thomas was rattling around on the second-floor level, and it dawned on me there was no place to stand out there. I wondered if he was lifting up.

"Say something mean to me, Missy," he commanded, grinning.

"Why? I can't think of anything mean to say to you, Old Thomas," I said.

"Go on. You can't hurt me."

So I thought awhile. The only words that came out were "fat slob," because those were words my brother said that hurt me, and even though I said them right back at him, he wasn't fat, so I didn't think it hurt him so much. But right there my mouth turned into a shotgun and I spat those words into the air like they were fireballs from a Roman candle. When they hit Old Thomas in his padded white armor suit, they fizzled out and slid to the floor and burned to a crisp nothing, only a pile of cool gray ash. I looked at Old Thomas, so amazed I just said, "Wow, that was great!"

"See? Now say something nice, Missy," he said. That was easy. I said, "I love you, Old Thomas," and those words transformed into rose petals and flew through the air in circles, and his fuchsia heart grabbed each letter and hugged it and hid each one in a cumulus cloud, and right away I asked if we could do it again, but before we did, I woke up because Mother came in to shut my window. The blinds, blowing together, were making a loud noise as wind picked up for a thunderstorm.

A few weeks later, on a Sunday, I went with Old Thomas to the Lolololo tree again. The Sunday adventures got pretty regular for us in those days when Old Thomas rose up in activity, bustling around, feeding and conversing with each of his strange friends, lifting up a bird's wing, poking a sleeping snake with a stick to wake him, peeking in the O-holes to see how many were in residence. The whole time he was humming, nothing was familiar to me. But this particular Sunday there was a basket bedding a camel-colored wild cat with a pink nose who showed his teeth and hissed every time I got close. I could see he didn't feel too good—there was an awful-looking bullet wound in his shoulder. The baby colts, which stayed in the back pasture, came in close to graze and frolicked with the airmail birds that were riding on their ear points. The mothers ignored us. They were busy nuzzling their noses through deep grass for chicory leaves. They all were accustomed to Old Thomas. The bravest colts rubbed their cheeks on us, and I knew they hoped for peppermint candies we sometimes brought in our pockets.

Robertelee didn't always come with us, but that day he was there, and he was quieter than usual. I think maybe he sensed Old Thomas had something to say as he lit a partly smoked cigar and breathed in deeply while we settled on the old stumps he always arranged for us.

Everything was silent except the noises left over from the insects in the grasses.

"Thought maybe I'd tell you the story of the first Blue Racer and how he got his stripes," Old Thomas said.

We always knew when we were going to hear a special story by the way he pinched his nose near his eyes to draw up his memory and then folded himself so he was sitting on his heels and humming those strange, soft sounds. This one, he told us, was a transformation story with a surefire pilgrimage built in. He said Blue Racer was born right here, beneath the roots of our tree, but back then he was just this friendly, harmless green snake who resembled the grasses he slid among. Come late August, just past picking time, when the farmers were battling the boll weevils that infest cotton bolls, the green snake was elected King of the Cotton Makers' Jubilee Snake Competition.

We didn't know what that was, but Old Thomas explained that white folks have Cotton Carnival and coloreds have the Cotton Makers' Jubilee, and on that day snakes of all diversities hold a celebration to elect an elder snake to lead them on. Well, when the poor green snake won that year's elections, he had to consider his potential. He wasn't experienced. He wasn't besieged by wisdom. He wasn't particularly handsome. He wished he were all those things, Old Thomas said, but he looked just like all the other thin green snakes in the land.

My brother interrupted—he wanted to know if Old Thomas was at the snake competition.

"Yessirree, I was," Old Thomas said. "I even pointed out to the new King Green he had on himself a couple God-given talents: he sang convincing as a rooster for sunrise. Suppose it was snake gospels he chanted, since he was a note caller and churches solicited him for tunin' up choirs."

I was getting older, and age was failing to suspend my disbelief, so I wanted more facts before I could believe anything, and I told Old Thomas that, and he wiped his face, which was black as potting soil, with that large white handkerchief he always kept in his back pocket, and he settled in to tell us what I knew was going to be a long story, and an important one.

He told us the chairman snake for many carnivals before that one had been the loquacious and dangerous Elder Cottonmouth. One snap of his pointed teeth would get any snake's attention because whenever he opened his mouth, he flashed a pound of gold on his teeth. He was crookeder than most, but he passed on some tips to the green snake. He said if he was going to take on being snake leader, he would have to go on a pilgrimage, and that meant leaving the Lolololo tree and going out to seek the gold bars of wisdom and salvation.

"Those can only be got from the Great Anaconda of the Amazon," Old Thomas said. He said it like we ought to know that. And he said many kings-elect had set out on that pilgrimage and because of that the snake population was thinning out, because none of those snakes came back in to tell what they'd found.

I could just see how Elder Cottonmouth was happy as could be, because as long as those green snakes didn't return, he would remain the Boss Man.

Now I noticed that the sun was filtered out by a distant grove of magnolia trees, and not too far off weanlings reclined with legs folded under their stomachs. Airmail birds rested their beaks on nest edges close to Old Thomas. All the O-holes had tongue-flicking snakes peering out, and I could see Frightnin' usually wasn't too comfortable being in such close quarters with the birds he liked to chase and the snakes he liked to grab in his teeth, but when Old Thomas told a tale, he told it in many languages, so everyone understood, and this time even Frightnin' was listening closely.

The newly elected King Green packed his bags and set out. Of course, he didn't know if he'd ever see his brothers again or if he'd come back with the ribbons and bars of a hero, but he was brave enough to hitch himself a ride in a cotton wagon toward the riverfront, figuring he would ride a barge down the river to New Orleans.

A couple days went by, and no barges passed, so King Green slid into the river. It seems he had picked up swimming by accident when he once pushed through a pile of cattails down by the pond. He fell in on ground that was supposed to be there but wasn't—like a lot of things in life, Old Thomas said. And he made the best of the situation, treading water with his tail and discovering this new talent that now was going to come in handy.

And so the tides pushed him along, and for weeks he moved down and against the river rapids, around barges, paddle wheelers, and tugs. Finally he brushed close to the coral reefs of Cuba, where, Old Thomas said, the white snakes wore white suits and Panama hats and the water smelled of tobacco, and the Cubans mistook him for an itinerant evangelist and convinced him to perform in a revival, and since he had to sing, he came up with a ballad:

Just a snake in the grass on a trip
Belly bound to the ground with a whip
Took the plunge pushin' forth on life's road
Headed out with a shout to find soul.
Now I quiver for a bar of gold for my mouth.
Only God knows the route I must take.
Hurry on, my salvation's at stake.

And after the applause he slid out of the Cuban port and back into the cool Caribbean and out into the Atlantic, and when a couple of moray eels met him, they gave him some advice that helped him latch onto the currents of the Amazon, and that lifted his spirits. So far most had smiled warmly when they'd seen him skimming their borders, and he figured maybe the world wasn't so frightening. And after that, the newly elected King Green always smiled.

I knew Old Thomas was telling us a kind of metaphor, but I also knew this story was important, and I leaned in closer and listened harder as he described King Green's decision to rest on the banks of the Amazon, where he marveled at the size of that river. He couldn't even see the other side. But as he rested there under the Brazilian sun, his skin's natural emerald tint was restored—it had grown brown in the Mississippi—and for the first time he analyzed himself, and he saw that he had doubled in size and muscle since he'd left home, and he liked that. He lay back to catch up on some sleep, when he heard a screech like a loose tractor belt, and when he lifted his head he saw a strange black bird with a banana-yellow beak, and in that beak was a flopping fish.

When Old Thomas said that, the airmail doves pushed forward in their nests, and I knew they liked their part of the story because a bird had shown up in it. I knew a little bit about the Amazon because we made clay maps of South America in school, so I already knew it was bigger than the Mississippi, but Old Thomas knew a lot more—he knew an awful lot of geography for someone who had been no farther off than Memphis.

Now he was talking like all the animals. *"Bem vindo. Todo bem, todo bem."* That's what the bird said, and he poked his beak into King

Green, who grew aware of a beat pulsing in the air everywhere around him—a rhythm he couldn't quite explain. And Yellow Bird told him that he was the toucan in the promised land, and that he hoped Green Snake wasn't just one more Mississippi brother with jelly eyes.

Toucan split from his perch and took off for a palm tree and set to humming through the sides of his beak, so King Green cleared his throat and rode up on the rhythm of that voice, and he set off in harmony to Toucan's melody, and together, Old Thomas said, they sounded like the Ink Spots. I could hear doo-wop in the air around us as soon as Old Thomas mentioned them.

Toucan flew around, gathering up bananas, pineapples, mangos, melons, papayas, and placing all of those on his head, like Carmen Miranda, and King Green told him he was on a pilgrimage to find the Great Anaconda, the biggest snake of the species, who dispenses wisdom and gold bars for teeth. He said his soul drove him so he didn't have to know the route. He said it was being taken for him. And that's when Toucan told him about all the powerful creatures he was bound to cross—like Piranha and Crocodile—even before he found the Great Anaconda.

Now, King Green had chickenhawk experience from back at the Lolololo tree, or at least he said that because he didn't want Toucan to think he was ignorant, but Toucan laughed and explained that Crocodile's mouth was like a Cadillac car hood that could snap shut faster than a booby trap and could grab anything in between its teeth and tonsils.

King Green tried to settle into some semblance of peace, and when he did, without noticing, he let the tail end of his body slip into the water, and a few minutes later he was aroused from his nap by agitations on the water's surface, and then he felt something clamp onto his tail, and Toucan told him he'd just met Piranha.

King Green whipped his sore tail and tore out of there, but the Piranha followed him. Luckily he was faster, and so he sped on, and the jungle grew thicker and greener and taller and noisier and fiercer and dirtier and more crowded with strange underwater creatures. And when King Green got hungry, he slithered up a rocky bank and found a stack of motherless white eggs.

Naturally, he grabbed at one egg and broke it open with his new-and-improved body. He was just beginning to enjoy the taste, when the ground vibrated, and one rock, bumpy as an egg carton, turned into a beast that moved toward him with the speed of a racehorse. He dived into the water, but Crocodile splashed in right behind him, and they charged along the surface of the Amazon, and somehow King Green outraced that croc, and when he finally reached safe land, he heard beaky Toucan overhead and he saw him flying in figure eights, and a congregation of birds were all around, and Toucan cried, "Grand *Señor* Green, Superman of the Jungle, what's your *formulario*? How do you do it?"

But King Green didn't know, and it was Toucan who had to tell him that a whole pool of piranhas were curled up with stomach cramps, and evil Crocodile was devastated at having lost the chase, and that's when King Green felt himself being lifted up and carried along through damp webs of grass. A parade of creatures were carrying him. They carried him to a strange and wonderful tree covered in pink, mauve, and purple orchids, thousands of them hanging suspended, branches dipping from the weight of the flowers, and at the base of the trunk was a carpet of pink petals as thick as a mattress. The very exhausted King Green thought it looked like a great cushion to fall on, and then he saw, there in the air, folded up in the branches like a complicated pretzel, its body thick as a telephone pole, the Great Anaconda, the biggest snake in the world.

He had a mouth full of green apples and a powerful hold on things because he could easily just strangle opposition. He was surrounded by hundreds of lesser snakes. But King Green didn't think about protocol. He didn't bow or wait to be spoken to or anything. He just started talking about the Bible legends he knew about him, about the apple man who tempted Adam to eat his way out of the beautiful kingdom of apple trees.

The anaconda shifted and squirmed and rearranged the curls and curves and circles and twists, making sure his admirers saw his pretty self. He hypnotized his gallery with that samba beat that gave King Green a headache, but when Anaconda invited him, King Green moved closer and whispered, "Let's get it over with. I've got to end this pilgrimage and win that bar of gold for my teeth and prove I've found wisdom."

Great Anaconda had a wicked laugh that made King Green restless to get out of there. From ground level, he squinted to take in all being given out, and then Great Anaconda invited King Green to slide on up his tree, to wrap around a bougainvillea branch, to get a feel for the situation and join the luxury up there, where he could have all the treasures he wanted—silver stripes or brass earrings or any kind of jewel—if he would just live with Great Anaconda and be his apprentice. If he did that, everything Great Anaconda had would be King Green's, too, and Great Anaconda would promote him as the fastest snake in the jungle, and he'd even organize croc races.

But King Green said he wasn't looking for trouble, and his heart pumped a hard beat as he remembered the close calls he'd had. He was feeling homesick, and he tried to explain he really was just a simple snake, and all he wanted was the wisdom he needed and a bar of gold to cover his teeth, and he would be done with his pilgrimage and he'd go back home.

But Anaconda wanted a closer peek at this fellow, so, keeping on his toes, King Green pushed closer, even though he knew what Great Anaconda might do to him in the face of this rejection. An assistant snake, a copper-and-silver diamondback, handed the Great Anaconda a seed pod that looked like a Ping-Pong ball and crushed it open. A spray of sapphire blue and silver powder sprang out, scattering all over the instantly beautiful King Green's damp emerald body.

King Green had no idea what had happened, but Great Anaconda told him he was knighting him Champion King Green, the fastest snake between two points, and from that day on he would wear silver and blue racing stripes as a mark that he was the first in line to be known as the Blue Racer, OBE, PhD, FBI, KOA. And he put gold bars on King Green's teeth.

All the snake audience clapped their tails against the giant tree, and Toucan sang into the chest of his sidekick, "Now and forevermore the Blue Racer. Amen."

And a great cheer rose, and then everyone fell silent.

And Blue Racer King Green smiled in his modest way and slowly backed down the path, seriously eager to get back to the Mississippi River and to the Lolololo tree. I understood that. The Lolololo tree and the river were where I always wanted to be, too.

Old Thomas said Blue Racer King Green wasn't worried about the return trip. A whole bunch of admirers had geared up to accompany him, and so the newly wise blue-and-silver racing snake had done everything required of any serpent soul. When Old Thomas finished, for the first time I noticed something I'd never noticed about him. Old Thomas had gold bars on his teeth.

Ten

W e begged Mammyrosy to let us go play with B-Budd again, but she just shook her head and said, "Something snapped in that white boy's mind a long time ago, and he ain't actin' ordinary no more, not since he left that crazy hospital." And when Mammyrosy didn't want us doing something, there was no getting around her.

By that time B-Budd had been home a few months, and we kept begging, but she kept insisting Miss Lucy (that's what she called Mother) didn't want us hanging around down there. "No sirree. It's dangerous, that child walking around with his BB gun locked under his armpit like a third arm. Too much shootin'. Too dangerous for my young'uns. I can't believe Mr. Hugh would let his boy go around with a gun after all that's happened."

But I knew B-Budd wasn't dangerous. He didn't get along much with animals, but he was okay with me. I even think he liked me special, and I was tired of waiting. So one day I convinced Robertelee with a couple of chewy Clark bars that it was time to go visit, and without saying a word to Mammyrosy or asking anyone's permission, we set out on our bicycles down that long winding drive to the front of the farm. We tried to seem casual as we rode so if anyone saw us we wouldn't look like we had any plan in mind. We sneaked up behind the house on the chicken coops to count how many chickens had heads. When those chickens saw us, they snapped their heads from one side to the other as if they expected something horrible was about to happen. But B-Budd wasn't there, so we moved on over to the screened porch, and when we got there I put my bike down and knocked on the wood part of the door. It gave in each time I hit it, so one knock was like two. "B-Budd? B-Budd?" I called.

Mrs. Hugh, her hair drawn up in a messy knot with a lot of wisps escaping, like Marjorie Main from the Ma and Pa Kettle movies I liked to watch, was as big as Sheriff Ferget, and she came to the door carrying a load of fresh brown eggs in her apron, holding the ends up so the eggs wouldn't roll out. In her duck-quack voice she told us B-Budd wasn't feeling good. She didn't even unlatch the door.

If I squinted hard enough past the screen door, I could see B-Budd's silhouette far back in the dining room. He was sitting in a fold-up lawn chair. He was as long as it was. His hair, white as rice, was still in a crew cut. That's how I was sure it was him. I'm sure he could see us, but he didn't say anything, not even a wave, and from where I was standing there didn't seem to be much of him there. He was holding his pocketknife in the air and saying psalm verses. I could see his pet snakes sitting like rolled-up tape in their cages right beside the screen door.

I leaned around his mother's large body and yelled enthusiastically, "Hi, B-Budd."

"Go on now, children," his mother said, moving so I couldn't see. "Mr. Georgelea won't like you being down here."

"Why can't B-Budd come play? Is he sick?"

"He done got himself bit by a water moccasin," she said, juggling those eggs a little so I was afraid she might drop them. "He's got to stay in bed until the poison works its way out before it gets to his head."

"How do you get rid of that?" I thought I might have to ask Old Thomas, and I wondered if B-Budd's mother knew how to fix him. She didn't want to answer me, though. She just told me to go on home. "I can't talk about it no more, and you stay away from that pond, ya hear? And don't say nothing to nobody. Yo mama's going to be mad if she knows you come down here."

We turned around and rode away, but all the way home Robertelee kept saying, "Wow-wee, wow-wee," and I knew now more than ever I had to work out a plan to cure B-Budd. Strange ideas came to me like june bugs flying around, and those strange ideas kept giving me solutions, ways to fix B-Budd. Whenever I could I collected a mixture of beechos and the red hearts that popped out of my knee, and I put these in a sack I hid in my room. I got two barbecue ribs with meat chewed off them, and a little sack of cotton flakes I picked up from under the cotton trees in the far back pasture, and I put those in there, too. The only thing I hadn't figured out was how to get B-Budd to come with me to where I wanted to lead him, and how to make sure Mammyrosy didn't get in our way.

And then one day a month after our visit, we were driving in the gate, coming home from school, and as we passed the chicken coop, I saw him standing there, and I shouted, "B-Budd's well!" and Robertelee shouted it, too, and so I promised myself I was going to sneak away to see him as soon as I could.

On Saturday morning Robertelee and I casually walked into the kitchen, where Mammyrosy was sitting in a too-small chair, polishing silver. I thought she was concentrating hard and that we could sneak out, but the minute I opened the door she looked up and said, "Where you two headin'?"

"Oh, down," I said.

"Down to what?" she asked. "I know you two are gearin' up for some mischief. My heart's a-tremblin'."

I stopped and looked at her, and with as serious a face as I could force up, I said, "Mammyrosy, B-Budd got bit by a snake. He knows all about snakes. And he told me snakes know a religious person, so I don't think that poison did one iota of bad to him."

"That boy is bad medicine," Mammyrosy said.

I knew my feelings and statement were bold, but I also knew I had to try my plan quickly, before something else happened. I figured if I could get B-Budd up to the back pasture near the Lolololo tree, I could get things done without his ever even seeing the Lolololo. I was sure of it. That meant I wasn't exactly breaking my promise to Old Thomas about keeping it all secret. The thing was, it looked like I was B-Budd's only friend, so it was up to me to try to save his heart.

"We won't be long," I said as fast as I could, and Robertelee and I sped out of there—too fast for Mammyrosy to stop us. When we got to the chicken coop on our bikes, B-Budd was there, chasing after those poor chickens. They squawked and squealed and flapped their feathers, in a real fright, I could see. The girls had little families of fuzzy chicklets following them around while they tried to escape, and whenever they got under B-Budd's thick-soled boots, he smashed down on them without even noticing he did and he yelled out, "Daughter of Babel, a blessing on anyone who seizes your babies and shatters them against a rock."

I stood there watching for a few seconds, before I yelled, "Hey, B-Budd, whatcha doing? Can we help?" I was trying to seem as normal as possible, like nothing had ever happened, but B-Budd didn't even look up.

When he did finally turn around, I saw he was holding an ax in one hand and a chicken in the other. "In prosperity people become no better than dumb animals," he shouted, and he laid the poor chicken's neck across a wooden stump, and before I could even turn away, he brought that ax down. I heard a loud crack and then a horrible silence, and the chicken's sweaty body, minus its head, the feathers plastered to the skin with blood that gushed out of its neck, began to run in circles.

B-Budd chased after it, and when he reached it he grabbed the body and held it upside down by its yellow feet.

That's when he looked over at me and smiled.

I couldn't take my eyes off the blood pouring out of that neck. It looked to me like B-Budd's front side had grown twice as tall as it had been when he used to frog-gig, but his face was vanilla white. "B-Budd," I said, but I didn't know what else to say now, and he didn't say a word to me. He just looked out into space. And then he said, to nobody in particular, "All who hate me whisper together about me and reckon I deserve the misery I suffer." Then he turned back around to chase another fleeing chicken.

"Are you talking to me, B-Budd?" I asked, a little louder. "I don't hate you. I've never hated you. I'm your friend."

It was coming clear he wasn't thinking like I thought thinking happens, and I knew I was going to have to move fast.

"I want to show you something, B-Budd," I said. "Something good. It's a place where there's a whole bunch of snakes that do magic things. We've got to take a ride on our bicycles to see it. Come on. There's a whole bunch of snakes—"

"I have not sinned with my mouth, as most people do," B-Budd said.

"Listen to me, B-Budd. I know about some spiritual snakes, green and blue ones. They're helping snakes that do kind deeds, and they can help you be the way you used to be. Don't you want to come?"

"May Yahweh cut away every smooth lip, every boastful tongue!" he said, his voice growing louder.

I could see I wasn't getting anywhere, but I couldn't give up. "B-Budd, look, I can show you beechos and roots growing in a place you know nothing about. I bet we can find you a new name with magic in it so you'll never be sick again."

I'd almost forgotten all about Robertelee, but now I saw he was looking at me like I'd lost my head, and I knew he didn't understand.

"I'm a worm, not a man, scorn of man. All who see me jeer and sneer and wag their heads." B-Budd was shouting by then.

I was running out of things to say, and my brother had his nose poked through the chicken wire around the coop, watching the poor hens scatter up and down the ramps. And then, suddenly, B-Budd just opened the gate and left it wide open. He started walking down the road, but he kept yelling out things from the Bible.

I turned to Robertelee and shouted, "Shut the gate! Don't let the chickens escape."

He shut it, just in time, and we hopped on our bikes and rode. Sometimes we were behind B-Budd, who at least was heading in the right direction, and sometimes we rode in front—I thought we could lead him. I was determined to somehow steer us to the back pasture without passing near the big house. But B-Budd was so tall and straight and his crew cut was so white and stiff, he could have been a beacon in a fog, and besides that, he kept that ax head up under his arm, and I was afraid someone was going to see us before we reached the back pasture.

But he followed us then, and we dropped our bikes and crawled over the final fence, and suddenly B-Budd stopped. We stopped, too. There was silence all around us, so much silence, I almost felt as if we were underwater. And then a cluster of clouds thick as grease came right down to ground level, and I lost my direction. I looked around, but all I could see were those clouds.

Still, I figured we could head to the fence line, to the cotton trees Old Thomas had planted there.

But B-Budd kept going straight.

I scooted up ahead of him and turned around and said, "No, B-Budd, we can't go that way yet," but he ignored me and just kept on walking. Even the tall grasses wrapping around his legs like vines didn't slow him down. I tried to grab his hand, thinking maybe I could turn him around, but he still didn't stop, and when we came upon the broccoli stalks, I began to shake because that meant the Lolololo was in the distance, but B-Budd just kept walking.

"What am I going to do, Robertelee?" I asked. "B-Budd won't pay any attention." I figured maybe even my little brother could have an idea, but before he could think of an answer, B-Budd just disappeared into the clouds. I couldn't see him anymore, and I began to panic.

"Robertelee, we've got to go to the Lolololo. We've got to make sure B-Budd doesn't find it. I've made a terrible mistake. Old Thomas is going to kill me."

And then, just as fast as he had disappeared, B-Budd was there, heading back in our direction, but he'd lost his ax. Now he was carrying a shotgun covered in dried manure, and he held that gun way out in front of himself, both his arms extended. I was pretty sure that was the shotgun I'd heard about at Bozos, and I thought maybe B-Budd had pulled it out of the ground.

B-Budd kept moving forward, so stiff and scary, he looked like Frankenstein, and I turned to Robertelee and whispered, "I think the tree is safe, don't you?"

He nodded, and I dug my hand into my pocket and felt the red hearts and the rib bones and the crumbling beechos there. We followed B-Budd until we were sure he was heading back home. From a little ways away, we saw him walk into the chicken coop, but we didn't follow him inside this time. I just wondered what Mr. Hugh would say when he found out B-Budd had traded his ax for a stinky shotgun.

Eleven

After that Robertelee and I made a pact that we would never go to the Lolololo tree again if Old Thomas wasn't with us, but just a few days later, on one of those languid summer afternoons, clouds threatening rain, everything still as a photograph, we spent the entire afternoon exploring the back pasture, picking up some cotton flakes and playing a sort of tag with the green snakes. We knew it wasn't the right place to be, at least without Old Thomas, but we liked just being near and smelling the jasmine and watching the injured snakes slipping over that way.

Frightnin' had gone off with Redduddy to Bozos, and Old Thomas was busy down at the picnic shed with Mother, preparing for the annual compress picnic that was coming up on Saturday. Everyone was worried it might rain, so Robertelee and I created a "no rain" dance, like the Apache Indians' rain dance I'd read about.

All of a sudden I saw a beautiful green snake with colored stripes around his stomach and gold on the top of his head. I stooped to look closer and saw he had long, thick eyelashes. "Maybe it wants an O-hole," I said to Robertelee, and then, at that moment, without a warning, somebody grabbed me around my waist and lifted me up off the ground. The snake slipped out of my hands and disappeared in the grass.

It took me a few seconds to think to turn around and look, but when I did I saw three ugly men with big arms and black beards. They were dressed in checkered jackets with sleeves rolled up high and workers' boots. I'd seen two of these monsters before. They had tried to arrest Old Thomas, and now they were trying to carry us away.

"You kids tell us where that nigger's tree is. We ain't gonna let you go until you do," the ugliest of the three uglies said.

I was bent over in a V at the waist. I squirmed and kicked and hit his thighs, and Robertelee started yelling, "Help! Help!" But we knew no one would hear us way out there in the back pasture.

"How come you rascals take up with a nigger?" the ugliest man asked. "Don't you know niggers is contaminating and dangerous?" He was having a hard time holding me against his hip, but I felt his grip grow tighter.

"Let me go." I kicked so hard my jeans unsnapped. I punched a fist on my knee where the three rocks were, and right away I popped out of his hold, and I picked up a stick and began to hit the man holding my brother. "Let him go."

"Hey, sister," the man shouted, "stop it! Damn, that hurts."

The man who had grabbed me had big fat arms covered with drawings, and all three stank like whiskey. The one in the orange hunting jacket was still holding my brother, but just as I lifted the stick to hit him again, a phalanx of snakes wrapped themselves around the men's legs. Two of them tumbled down, but the one in the orange jacket was still standing in a pose, holding Robertelee up in the air by his belt, and then, before I could even register what was happening, Old Thomas was running toward us as fast as he could.

Out of the corner of my eye, I saw him jump at the man holding Robertelee. He grabbed that belt and shook my brother free. He and the man fell to the ground, Old Thomas on top.

"Off me," the man yelled, "I don't want no black skin on mine."

Old Thomas pushed my brother into the long grass in the direction of the big house, and suddenly I was running beside my brother. Behind us we could hear those men whopping Old Thomas with their sticks, shouting awful things, beating the snakes. I pulled Robertelee by the hand as hard as I could so he would keep up with me, and to take his mind off all those terrible things behind us, I said, "Let's race," and just then, faster than a tooth pull, a couple of blue racers slid in front of us, smoothing down the high grasses to lead us away. When we got to the cut-grass lawn that surrounded the big house, they disappeared.

"Daddy, Daddy!" I yelled, running inside, through the kitchen, dodging Mammyrosy's towel—she was trying to swat at us. We raced right into the den, where Daddy and Mother were reading magazines. "Daddy, something awful's happened to Old Thomas."

Mother gasped. "What in the world have you two been up to? Look at you—look at your clothes. You're about to earn yourselves a good spanking."

Daddy got up out of his chair. "Daddy." I looked into his eyes. "Daddy, these ugly, nasty men tried to hurt us. They hung Robertelee by his belt."

"There were snakes and everything." Robertelee was breathless, too. "Missy hit them with a stick." He grabbed Mother around the waist.

"They got Old Thomas, Daddy. They got him and they're trying to hurt him," I said. I was starting to cry, and Robertelee, holding Mother with all his might, burst into tears.

"Daddy, Old Thomas is in trouble. He really is," I said, trying to stay strong. I had to save Old Thomas. "Hurry, we have to save him." I tugged at his arm, but Mother shook her head and said, "Old Thomas just came up from the picnic shed after me. I'm sure he's all right."

"No, Mother, Old Thomas is in trouble," I said. "Old Thomas saved our lives—he pushed those men away so we'd come home— but we have to go save him."

"He did, Mommy—he pulled me out of that ugly man's arms," Robertelee said through his sobs.

"Now, now. You'll be all right." Mother pressed down on Robertelee's hair, but I was watching Daddy's face. I could see he was getting angry. "Goddammit," he said, "those sons of bitches have gone too far this time. How'd they get on the property? I have electric wires on all the fences. Where'd they find you kids?"

"We were out in the back pasture, playing crocodiles," I said, pretending innocence. It wouldn't do to tell him everything.

He stormed out of the den and out the back door, muttering, "Trespassing, pure trespassing. I'm sick and tired of the harassment. Get the sheriff on the phone."

Still playing with Robertelee's hair, Mother moved to the phone and dialed the sheriff's office, but I could see from her face no one was answering, and a few minutes later Daddy walked back inside, his face even redder, and he said, "Something's wrong—now I feel it. Why isn't Reddaddy back yet?"

"It's Thursday. He goes out to Bozos with the hounds and the sheriff," Mother said.

"Did you reach Sheriff Ferget?"

"No answer," she said, and I could see it was suddenly occurring to her that wasn't right; the sheriff always answered his calls.

"Call the emergency number and get his deputies over here. Now!" Daddy commanded. Still comforting my brother, Mother dialed the phone again and handed it over to Daddy.

"Get over here, Dub," he practically shouted into the phone. "Someone tried to kidnap the children, and I think they got Old Thomas. Go search the back pasture."

When he hung up, he looked at Mother. "You all stay inside the house, ya hear me?"

I didn't want to stay inside, but I could see Daddy was serious, so I promised, and so did Robertelee. Then Daddy got on the phone to Miss Lulu, and I could tell she was telling him Reddaddy wasn't there anymore. Daddy said, "I'm on my way," and when he hung up he said to Mother, "Reddaddy heard gunshots, and his hounds were acting crazy."

Then Daddy ran out the back-hall door with his car keys in hand, and Mother walked fast behind him. Robertelee and I followed her.

"Oh dear, Georgelea, we'll wait dinner for you. The children can have a sandwich."

"How in God's name can Reddaddy be running around those

hills, chasing hounds?" Daddy said, mostly to himself. "I warned him. That heart of his."

Mother seemed to notice us again, and she turned to me and said, "Missy, you and your brother get upstairs and into the tub. Put on your nightclothes, and you can come back down to have a cheese sandwich."

But I didn't listen. I just kept following Mother, who was following Daddy out to the back door. When I turned around, I saw Mammyrosy looking like the cross on a rosary, with her arms stretched out. She looked at me. "Missy," she said, "come give me some sugar," and I ran into her arms because I needed Mammyrosy's hug in that moment. She hugged me hard.

"Do you think Old Thomas is okay?" I whispered. "Those ugly men were calling him terrible things."

"Lordy, Missy, just close your ears. It's a horrible thing how some people talk to coloreds."

I looked up at her. I could feel those tears starting to fall down my face, but it was okay to let Mammyrosy see. "They beat Old Thomas," I said. "I saw them. And they put a sack on his head. I'm not lying. It's the truth."

"Don't worry your pretty little forehead. Yo Daddy will get to the bottom of this. Ooh-wee. That old tree. It's gettin' complicated."

I always knew I could say things to Mammyrosy that I couldn't say to Mother. At least she'd listen and seem to believe me, and now that I had her attention, I had to ask if we would find Old Thomas again. I needed her to know those men tried to make me show them the Lolololo tree but that they walked right through and never even saw it. I needed to know, so I asked her. "That tree is magic, ain't it, Mammyrosy?"

She shook her head at me. "What in the Lord's name were you doing out there without Old Thomas?" I could see by the look on her face she didn't want me to answer. "I should turn you over my lap and whup you," she said, but instead she just hugged me harder.

I could hear the sirens of the deputies' cars as they drove right across the field into the back pasture. I stood out back and watched and saw they had to get out and walk once they got to the fence. I could see the flashlights like lightning swords against the sky. I just stayed where I was.

It was a while before the deputies came to the back door. Mother met them there, and I stayed where I was so I could hear and see everything. The deputy told Mother they had seen there was a skirmish. They said they saw a bunch of dead snakes on the ground and a trail of boot prints heading outside the electric fence, so they followed the footsteps and found where the wires had been snipped, and there were deep tire tracks there, so they thought the kidnappers had escaped. They were sending out word to Memphis.

Mother was calm. "Thank you, gentlemen. Mr. Georgelea and I appreciate your help. I am sure Mr. Georgelea will be talking to Sheriff Ferget any minute now."

Mammyrosy had started to hum one of her religious songs, but even then, even after she sat down in her chair, she let me come to her and sit in her lap. She kept on hugging me, and we rocked a bit, just the two of us, humming and praying for Old Thomas to get home safe and sound.

I saw dinner was warming on the stove for Daddy, and Mother said she thought he'd be home soon.

"Missy, you go take a bath," she said, and I realized I didn't have much choice. Sometimes I just had to obey.

Twelve

I took my bath and ate a cheese sandwich, and I tried to stall, hoping Daddy would come home with news of Old Thomas, but he didn't, and Mother finally sent me to bed at ten. I lay in my bed, but I couldn't sleep, and then, after a while, I heard a commotion in the kitchen, and I knew Daddy was home. I sneaked to the top of the stairs and looked down where I could see my parents, Sheriff Ferget, and Reddaddy sitting around the dining room table. Mammyrosy had stretched Daddy's meal, so everyone had something to eat. I wasn't sure what time it was, but I bet it was midnight.

"You are out of your head," Daddy said to Reddaddy. His face was stern, the way it always looked when he was being firm. "What possessed you to go up in those hills?"

Before Reddaddy could say a word, Sheriff Ferget stepped in. "Here's what's happened," he said, and that's when he told the whole story.

He said he and Reddaddy heard cracks like gunshots, and they heard the hounds beginning to scream like babies. Those hounds began to run in circles, so they chased them down to the ravine, and that's where they found Old Thomas's wool hat and Frightnin' whooping like a hyena. When the dog saw the sheriff, he grabbed the hat in his mouth and took off up into the hills, and Reddaddy and the sheriff chased him as best they could.

Then it started to rain, the sheriff said, and I leaned even farther over the banister because I had to hear every word the sheriff said. I was picturing Reddaddy out there in the rain, chasing those hounds. He said they were wetter than gnats swimming in a dipper and they were going to call it quits, when they came up a rise and saw a big cloud of steam coming up from a grove of trees, so they kept climbing. And that's when they came face-to-face with a band of men holding rifles.

Reddaddy talked about their eyes. He said they were red, like the devil's, but when the sheriff drew his pistol and held up his badge, they seemed scared.

There were a lot of men back there in the distance, but when they saw the sheriff arresting the three men, those others turned and jumped into a pair of old trucks that sounded like a herd of buffalo trying to escape through the trees.

Reddaddy was sure he had seen Mr. Hugh with those other men.

I wasn't sure I understood the whole story, but I understood when the sheriff said they found a homemade whiskey still that he knocked down with his hands, and I understood what it meant that old Frightnin' kept barking. Frightnin' almost never barked.

But then Frightnin' started loping along, and they followed him, and that's how they found Old Thomas. He was tied to an oak tree, and there were whiskey bottles and whips at his feet, and he had a sack over his head.

They untied him and carried him all the way back down the hill. They left him at his house with a deputy outside, just in case.

And when Daddy said how awful it was what had happened, the sheriff told him what I knew was true. He said he was only worried about Robertelee and me, and about being ready for the barbecue on Saturday.

And now those three kidnappers were in jail, and I was relieved to know Old Thomas was okay.

I must have fallen asleep there at the top of the stairs. I don't even know who carried me to bed later, but somebody did. And the next morning when I got up, Old Thomas was back on the farm, and everything seemed right again.

Later, when I was a little older, I heard another story about Old Thomas. Sheriff Ferget told me. He said some men had threatened to hurt Old Thomas if he didn't show them the magic potions he had holed up in the Lolololo tree, and those men beat him and tied him up in a tow sack and threw him into their pickup like he was a sack of wood chips, but he just hummed and went along with what was happening to him. He was sure he had special protection from the Lord.

The sheriff said they hauled him a long ways down some bumpy roads, but what Old Thomas didn't realize was that two dozen snakes had leaped aboard the pickup and were riding on its trim. The men didn't notice either, or maybe the snakes were invisible, but Old Thomas could feel their presence even when he didn't see them, and his hum blocked out all the ugly things the men were shouting and singing from the cab of the truck. He felt no pain. In fact, he was thinking about religious things, wondering if he'd be late for church.

When they reached the edge of the Mississippi riverbank, two of them lifted him out of the truck and, holding the tow sack by both ends, swung him as far as they could out into the fast and muddy waters down around Mud Island where the paddle wheelers and barges parked. But even then Old Thomas didn't consider his life over. He just called up some breathing exercises to keep his lungs going, and pretty soon he felt water moccasins biting at the sack, until they made a hole in it and he was able to look out into the water through his white eye. He saw schools of catfish swimming along beside him. They were making sure the tow sack didn't get caught in the current in the middle of the river, but even from underwater he could hear the men in their truck. They were cursing and cheering and slapping each other on the back, but a second later they were screaming, and Old Thomas knew those snakes had wrapped their extralong blue-and-green bodies around the men's appendages, and they were squeezing, and those tough guys screamed and shouted, but the docking area was empty, and the only thing that heard them was the air—and Old Thomas underwater.

A few miles down the river, Old Thomas's sack caught on a dead branch stuck into the mud right in the line of where he was flowing, and two pure-white egrets dropped down from the sky, ripped open the sack, and plopped him out like a cherry pit, and Old Thomas crawled out and rolled over onto the muddy banks, where he could hear the catfish slapping the waters in applause, and meanwhile a gang of green snakes had slid up out of the river muck to form a circle around Old Thomas's wet and curved form so he wouldn't slip back in. They made a tiny sound that could have been kin to Old Thomas's own peculiar hum. Sheriff Ferget said that's what convinced Old Thomas not to give up on life, and pretty soon he heard a hound dog barking like it had come upon a bear, but it was only the shiny green snake bodies generating light that disturbed that hound. It kept on barking, and when Old Thomas heard that, he knew he was still living and someone would surely show up. And, sure enough, two police recruits with flashlights slid down the incline to see what was bothering the old hound, and there was Old Thomas's limp body. They began to shout out to him, telling him Reddaddy and the sheriff were searching for him. They wrapped him up, and since he was heavy as a sponge in a waterfall, they had to drag him up the hill and get him an ambulance, but after that everyone who heard the story knew what I'd always known somehow: Old Thomas had some special angels.

And by the time Sheriff Ferget told me that story, I knew I had some angels, too.

That whole next week after Old Thomas was back home and everyone was getting ready for the barbecue, Mother kept calling herself a wreck and blaming it on trying to get things ready. She complained to Daddy that whenever she needed the servants to do things right, they did something ridiculous. That's how she put it. I ignored her because I thought that wasn't the least bit true, and Daddy ignored her, too, since she usually got in a nit fit before the picnic, because that was the time we showed off all thousand acres of the farm to everyone—to all his friends from Memphis and all Daddy's clients from everywhere around.

The picnic shed and the barbecue pits were permanent fixtures at the farm, shaded by trees so tall you'd have to stand on a roof to get to the first branch. One permanent brick barbecue pit was two times as long as the longest horse trough we had, but most of the time the barbecue area was in a state of falling apart. So each year before the big barbecue, it had to be spruced up because there in that brick barbecue pit, under sheets of tin, pork shoulders would be marinated in a gray fog. In another part of the area, a hole big enough for a quartet of bulls was freshly dug out of the ground and crude wire frames were stretched across to give hundreds of split yellow chickens a place to rest. Each of those chickens would be carved down the middle and stretched out so that one side looked like the other, and below them the orange and black coals, like rocks, would burn away, changing color the longer you watched.

On the morning of the big barbecue, we all gathered at the horse barn to walk out past the pond, a pasture's length away from the picnic area. Mother was fidgeting with my hair, warning me not to bother Reddaddy. She said he was worn out after all that had happened last week, and when I looked at him I saw his shirt was circled in rings of water, and he had his blue-and-white seersucker jacket folded over his arms, so I could see she was right. He did look worn out—his rosy cheeks and nose were creamy white, and his blue eyes were watery. I could see he was trying hard not to show how tired he was, but he was leaning on his cane, leaving holes in the grass.

Daddy was off with Sheriff Ferget, buying more ice blocks to put in the drinks, and Mother, wanting me to do something so I wouldn't bother her, sent me off to find Old Thomas. "See how he's feeling today. I bet he's at the barbecue pit with Big John," she added, before she walked over to greet some big fat man I didn't recognize who was coming up the road. He was wearing a hat like Daddy's and walking beside his wife, who was plain as pancakes without syrup.

I knew Old Thomas would be helping Big John like he always did, and I knew if I found him I'd get a sample of barbecue before everyone else, so Robertelee and I dashed off in a race with Frightnin' loping behind us, his ears flopping each time a foot hit the ground. Big John, the cook, had already been at it all night, basting, turning, moving, tasting. He had two helpers with him besides Old Thomas. Even then, though I was still just a child, I knew they'd all stayed awake by drinking bourbon whiskey out of a paper cup and talking, telling those stories they liked to tell, like the stories they later told me. Few people knew as much about barbecue religion as Old Thomas. Even with his bruises and bumps, he looked happy working that barbecue, but they almost ignored us, they were so busy. So I just studied them the way I liked to, especially Big John, who was a different color than the other colored men, as if someone had dropped a scoop of vanilla ice cream over him. He was taller than everyone else, too, with a watermelon stomach covered in stained aprons and long swabbing sticks in his hands. He was basting those chicken bodies, flopping each one over to its other side, and the fire spit and hissed as juice leaked down into it. Robertelee and I agreed it smelled even better than Daddy's chunk chocolate, which I wasn't allowed to have anyway. The whole farm began to smell like barbecue even better than Bozos.

Old Thomas was sitting on a chair near the pork shoulders, leaning with his elbow on his thigh, poking an extra-long fork over in the pork shoulder pits. I noticed his face looked a little gray. He had on his chewed-up cap, and a couple of airmail birds were getting a free rest beside him, like they were there to make sure he was okay. He was chewing on something that I was pretty sure must be beechos, since his lips were red. And even though it was steaming hot outside, he had a towel draped over his shoulders, like he might have been feeling cool. I guessed his back was hurting and he had to get warmed up before playing the piano like he usually did for the big barbecue.

I was glad to see he looked happy and fine, though, and after I was sure of that, I couldn't stop looking at Big John's shoes. He didn't wear these shoes down at the plant. The tongues hung out with no laces to hold them in, and they tilted down on the sides. They didn't look comfortable to me, since they had only half a sole, but he said those were his basting shoes, and he had to wear them when he was basting. Big John didn't speak much, especially when he was cooking, and he wouldn't tell anybody how to make his secret sauces. He just said that a marinade showed up in his head after he looked at what he had on the shelf.

The memory of those jars of his filled with sauce never went away: the copper-colored juices holding aloft squeezed lemon halves and chunks of transparent onion. Tiny sprinkle-dots of black and pumpkin orange floating around like sand swirling where ocean waves crashed. The end of a long stick swagged in a rag, closed up in the jar for a bit to soak up the juices, used for splashing the sauce on the chickens or pork shoulders. But that mostly came toward the end of cooking. When Big John unscrewed the tops of the glass gallon jars, like the ones coleslaw came in, the smell was more exciting than that of a new car with leather seat covers. Reddaddy said it was the best smell in the world, but I think that was because you could have it only once a year, and in between times you missed it.

And then came the best moment—the moment when I got to bite into the first rib. Robertelee and I knew we were special in those times, and we ate like we'd never eaten anything before in our lives, and we weren't thinking about any consequences of anything after that, until Mother showed up with a group of women.

The minute she was there, she marched over and said, "Missy, look at yourself—you're covered in barbecue sauce."

She was right, of course. I'd wiped my hands on my skirt and hadn't thought about it, and sweat was dripping down the backs of my legs, so I had rubbed the hem against my legs to stop it. The air was so hot, even my hair was perspiring. I didn't really care how I looked, but Mother did. Luckily, Reddaddy came up just then, and he smiled that Reddaddy smile and announced to all the guests, "Barbecue's browning!" And at that same moment Daddy and Sheriff Ferget arrived with plenty of ice to refresh the drinks, so Mother was distracted because she was trying to make everyone happy. So I got away.

The buffet tables outside the shed were loaded down with green and white coleslaw, yellow and white potato salad, black barrels of baked beans, and pink half-moon slices of watermelon with black teardrop seeds. As the chicken parts and pulled-pork pieces came off the barbecue shoulders, the table loaded up with them, and everyone filled a red-checked paper plate and sat down inside the shed. By then, even before I'd noticed it, the place had filled up with people from everywhere. Some of them knew each other, and some of them didn't, but it didn't matter if they didn't know each other because barbecue made everyone friendly, and even though it was hot, after a few bites of that chicken and pork, everyone forgot about that, too.

After a while I overheard a couple people asking Daddy if Old Thomas was going to play piano. "After all that happened," they whispered, but Daddy assured everyone that Old Thomas would have something special today. He announced that Sheriff Ferget had closed the case and everyone ought to have a good time. He put his arm around the shoulders of two cotton-plant superintendents, who smiled and nodded and agreed it was a good day to have a good time, and pretty soon they moved off to the table to load up their plates.

It wasn't too long before the jug band began to arrive just like they always did, right about the time the guests had filled their plates with seconds. I noticed Old Thomas kept falling off in a doze, but now that the jug band was there, he perked up and helped them set up at one end of the barn, and poured them each a full glass of whiskey while the white folks kept on eating barbecue.

After they were full of whiskey, the band members strolled to the edges of the dance floor, sat down on the wooden Coca-Cola crates Old Thomas had set up, and began to tune their instruments. I knew those band members from other years, like the tall, ancient man in a black suit, wearing dark glasses, who couldn't see. A hound dog a lot like Frightnin' was one-half step ahead of the man's carved wooden cane. His music came from a painted broomstick tied with a piece of fishing line and poked into an oil can, but when he plucked the line, it came up with a fine kind of music—a whine, but sweet. I knew the singing lady, Little Laura Dukes, who was not much taller than I was. At the bottom of her parenthesis legs she wore shoes like Minnie Mouse's, and her hair was designed in spit curls that seemed sealed to her head, little circles the size of a bubble-blowing ring. Her lips were painted red. I knew Beat Pete with a mouth that looked like it was kissing all the time—he played the brass horn, and Old Thomas told me he was Louis Armstrong's cousin, though back then I didn't yet know who Louis Armstrong was. There were two more men I didn't know—a skinny fellow with arms longer than his legs who played the harmonica, and a big man with a beard edged in gray sprinkles and wearing a jacket, its pocket linings hanging down in strings; he held a fiddle under his arm.

Someone had rolled out an upright piano for Old Thomas. It was a pretty incomplete piano—it had no back and no top, and all its wires were exposed like it was a being-fixed radio, and a couple keys didn't sound. But that didn't matter. Old Thomas could always make do with whatever he got, and when he tuned up those piano keys, everyone fell silent. Everyone had a feeling about what was coming next. I walked over to where Sheriff Ferget and Reddaddy were sitting on metal chairs under the shade of a big oak. I liked spending time with the two of them best of all. The sheriff said, "Nothing like a little jitterbug to help settle down these satisfied stomachs."

Standing bent, with his arms stretched down to the keys, Old Thomas breathed a hum, like a bagpipe pumping up. The jug players kept their eyes on him as he searched out a chord on the piano to match his hum. The blind man, balancing on the edge of the Coke case, started clapping a beat slow as the pour of thick molasses. Old Thomas nodded to the others one by one to show them where to pick up, and pretty soon he was shouting as loud as Mahalia Jackson, but no one could tell if he was on key. He played the piano jelly roll–style, stopping often to wipe his hands with a white handkerchief. His dry brown fingers, stiff as fat cigars, slid over the keyboard as if it were greased. The joints didn't move.

Old Thomas warmed up good. The band crawled along, slowly at the start, behind the leader, listening to the words he wanted to say, interpreting them, deciding if they liked what he was coming up with. Most of the time Old Thomas sang songs about going home, and when he sang, it was like he was making a down payment on one of those mansions in the sky they talk about in the Bible. As his voice slapped around in his throat, I knew he saw that heavenly home's door wide open in wait for him. Beside it would be St. Peter, and inside was Precious Jesus and a family reunion. A smile like an ivory keyboard with gold caps let pass the sounds Old Thomas created. His eyes rolled in a reverie of ecstasy. His shouts got gravelly and rough from chord strain, but that didn't stop him. His bald head shone like a halo on an angel, and then, halfway into the song, when he was already gone into those heavenly fields, the audience hollering, "Yea-a-a-a-ah," I saw Old Thomas transport every living body to other realms on high notes only God would recognize.

"YEA-A-AH!" everyone called, even us kids.

The syncopated stomping and swaying from his brothers in the band intensified the tempo, and every guest was speechless, focused, drawn in against all will. Souls were lifted up, and up, and up, all by beat, beat, beat, until the final sound of the last chorus drew us all as high as we could go.

"Ye-ah-ah-ah. Amen. Ah-*men*, *ah*-men."

As if an electric shock had been passed between every standing creature, all motion stopped, exhausted, spent, and there in that barn there was pure silence, except for fly buzzes near barbecue waste. Those tuned in could hear the echoing rhythms still riding on the barely moving air. It took an extended minute for life to revive.

"Whew!" some low voice whispered, ever so faintly.

"Praise God," another voice whispered, quiet as a garden fairy.

I noticed when Sheriff Ferget shifted his feet, his handcuffs jingled, and a howl came rolling out of Frightnin'. My brother, who had been sitting in the cradle of Frightnin's lying-down body, had pulled on his long ear, it seemed. Someone laughed, but hardly, and the blind man began to pick at his instrument, and someone cleared his throat, and then Little Laura rested on a husky low note, her eyes still shut, her head slowly nodding as if she waited upon the Holy Ghost to cue her.

And then, at last, she found a tone she agreed with.

Old Thomas ran a rag across his head with one hand, touched some concurring bass notes on the keyboard with the other, and now, one by one, the guests began to shift their feet, shaking out a knee, smoothing down a crinoline skirt with a quick hand press, stuffing a loosened shirttail back under a trouser belt. Breathing was restored. It was as if all of us had been somewhere, spent all we had, seen all we had to see, and had to touch ground to see if we were back.

The blind man picked up Little Laura's key. The base thumped. A harmonica wailed. Someone began slapping his thigh with a tickety sound.

I noticed Old Thomas cast an eye at Reddaddy in his straw boater. He was sitting strangely in his metal chair and holding on to his walking cane, propping it in front of him between his knees like a king on a throne. Frightnin' moved to his feet, but Reddaddy just smiled at Old Thomas. I could see he wanted the music to go on. So it did. The dance floor continued to shake with the weight of two-steppers, sliding and gliding to the surefire beat of the jug band. Those too stuffed with barbecue stood around the edges, arms crossed on their stomachs, hats a little crooked on their heads, faces a little red, commentating on the agility of the younger members of the party. Sheriff Ferget was one of these.

Little Laura Dukes, in a dress that seemed like it'd fit my rag doll, was high-stepping as she threw out her voice and pulled it back, finding notes that fit into the tune she was singing, and not looking at anyone, but maybe at some other place where she knew better folks.

The sun was hot. A lot of handkerchiefs were put to use on foreheads and necks. The moisture from all the perspiration pouring off the bodies of dancers could supply a steam room, and still no one wanted to stop. The band was getting better and better the more whiskey its members drank.

Sheriff Ferget stooped down on the ground to have a conversation with Reddaddy, and I moved closer because I wanted to hear and I couldn't hear a thing for the music.

"Reddaddy, please dance with me." I stepped closer still. "Let's do the boogie-woogie, like you promised. One time. Please. Please."

Reddaddy gave me that smile. "Well, Missy," he said, "I'm so full of Big John's barbecue, I could do with a little activity to help out my digestion. My old stomach doesn't work as good as it used to."

Reddaddy got up slowly, laying his cane on the side of the chair, and I gripped his hand, which felt cool somehow. I was as happy as I've ever been. I loved dancing with Reddaddy.

Then, just as we were moving out to the floor to dance, Daddy broke out of a tight group of men in shirt sleeves and walked up to us. "Reddaddy," he said sternly, "you have no business on the dance floor. You know your heart can't stand any more excitement."

"Don't worry, son. I won't overdo it. My granddaughter wants to boogie-woogie. What harm can a little fancy stepping do?"

I was so glad Reddaddy wanted to dance, I ignored Daddy. We stepped up to the floor, and Reddaddy took hold of both my hands and said, "Now follow me," and I watched the floor and Reddaddy's feet in his brown-and-white shoes. He tapped his foot twice, then put one in front. The music had nothing to do with the beat we were dancing to, but we twirled around, Reddaddy almost lifting me up off the floor. We tapped our toes, front and back, and Reddaddy swung me out like a yo-yo.

I looked over at the piano. I could see Old Thomas lifting his eyebrows up, like something bothered him. He slowed the rhythm he was playing, too, but when he saw me looking at him, he smiled deliberately and nodded, and I twirled back to Reddaddy.

"Do it again, Reddaddy, do it again," I said. "I love swinging like that." And we started the step again, his hands holding on to mine so tightly it almost hurt. He spun me out once more, and that's when I saw Old Thomas jump up from the piano as if he'd been burned, but by the time I turned around to spin back, Reddaddy was on the floor, stretched out with his hand over his heart like he might be saying the pledge of allegiance. Candy balls and silver quarters tumbled out of his pocket.

I just stood there, not knowing what to do, watching everyone moving so fast. Sheriff Ferget ran off to his squad car with its walkie-talkie, his hand pressed on his pistol holster so it wouldn't flop on his hip. I turned to ask someone what had happened. "Did Reddaddy slip?" I asked, but nobody answered. They just pushed me away—there were people lining up like stalks of corn, blocking out everything—blocking out even the sun. Blocking out me.

"Reddaddy, let me through," I said, trying to push back in, but no one paid any attention to me, and tears piled up in my eyes as I tried harder to push back through the people fence. That's when I felt an arm around my waist, and I saw that it was Old Thomas who had grabbed me and pulled me back. His chest was wet, and he smelled like cabbage cooking.

"Now, hold on, Missy. Jest hold on to Old Thomas. Your Reddaddy is mighty sick. That sun just got too hot on him."

I looked up at Old Thomas, and I begged him, "Make him well," because if anyone could fix things, I knew it was Old Thomas.

Old Thomas grabbed my hand, and we weeded our way through the shocked crowd. Most of them were so wet from sweating I could see their underclothes peeking through, but most of what I noticed was the silence, like before the bad parts in movies.

Finally, there was Reddaddy. His eyes were closed, and he was smiling, and someone had rolled up a jacket and put it under his head. Daddy was kneeling beside him, rubbing Reddaddy's forehead with a damp rag so that the red hair pushed back in a pompadour. Someone else had opened an umbrella and held it up to keep out the sun.

Next thing I saw, Sheriff Ferget backed Daddy's car into the picnic area as close as possible to the dance floor, and Big John and the trumpet man and a couple of others I didn't know helped to lift Reddaddy up and straight out like a mummy in a box, and they placed him delicately on the backseat of the car, right on top of my brother's gun and holster. Frightnin' leaped in, too, causing a disturbance, but Sheriff Ferget got out and pulled that dog out by the neck. "You can't go, Frightnin'," he said, and shut the door.

Daddy slipped into the front seat alongside Sheriff Ferget, and they drove off, leaving behind dust in big puffs to choke us.

I turned around and saw Old Thomas standing there. He'd turned me loose because it was over now, and he bowed his head for a minute, as if to get another wind, or maybe to say a prayer. I looked closely at him. I couldn't understand why someone who could cure all those snakes and birds couldn't fix Reddaddy, too, so I asked him why. He took my hand.

"There's some things, young'un, Old Thomas can't do unless the Lord Jesus tell him to. Sometimes it's better to leave things be. When our last day comes, we gets on wings and soar out of sight to join the saints. We knows how fine a saint Reddaddy is. We knows he's a genuine friend of Jesus. We knows he's the best man we'll ever know. But now he's going to another side of the sky. Over there people are waiting for him to get there, and he'll be the same to them as he was to us, maybe more."

I was listening hard, and I remember every word, but I didn't want to believe it was true.

"Now, Missy, I want you to look up in that sky. Look for your Reddaddy. He ain't left us yet. But he's bound to go any minute. I feel it in my soul. When you's got each other's blood, you knows the souls." He pointed his piano fingers up to the sky, between the giant oak trees, and I followed those fingers with my gaze. "Tell me, Missy," he said, "can't you see them angels flying up there? See the ones with the golden wings and golden shoes?"

I looked with all my strength. I trusted Old Thomas.

"I want you to keep looking up there toward the holy heavens," he said, "and when you see Reddaddy going by, wave to him. He'll smile to let you know he's fine."

I still couldn't see him, but I asked if I could yell to him. And if I could blow him a kiss, and Old Thomas said that would delight Reddaddy. "In fact," he said, "I wouldn't doubt if you'd get an air-mail bird to tote that kiss up there to him."

And then when I looked back down again, Old Thomas had just disappeared, and I felt more alone than I had ever felt in my life, like all my life had gone away. I sat down on the edge of the dance floor, brushing my hand through the grass that peeked up through the boards. The sun was beating down hard, and Frightnin' was pacing back and forth, sniffing the ground as if he were bound to find something. I'm sure there must have been some people left from the barbecue, but I don't remember seeing anyone at all—just me and Frightnin' looking up at the sky.

"Old Thomas said we have to look up in the sky, Frightnin'," I told him. "Reddaddy is gonna pass by in his angel costume and send us a kiss," I said, but Frightnin' began to whine. He pressed his nose to Reddaddy's cane, which was still leaning against the metal chair where Reddaddy had spent most of that day. I grabbed the cane up and held it to my chest, because now this was mine. I was sure

Reddaddy had left it for me, and I swore I'd keep it safe until his heart got fixed.

Frightnin' came over and laid his face across my leg, and I could feel him swallow, and I wondered if he thought maybe I was Reddaddy now that I had his cane.

A silver cloud bulging with rain drifted right over our heads, and thunder began to rumble. I wondered why the rocks in my knees were hurting and why my stomach felt bad. I wondered a lot of things while the rain poured down, but after the shower passed— and it was quick—a rainbow lifted up right over the pond, and a heap of green snakes lined up like matchsticks around the pond's edge. Their skins turned to rainbow colors—pink, yellow, blue—and then they slid back under the lily pads, and when they did I looked up at the sky, and I swear I saw Reddaddy passing by. I stood up and waved his cane, and I yelled out to him. "Reddaddy, I'm here. I love you. Blow me a kiss!" And a pair of airmail birds, their beaks and feet flossed in gold, flew down and brushed my cheeks with their white wings and flew straight up into the sky, to where Reddaddy was passing to another place. I saw him press his hands to their lips, and as he floated higher toward the rainbow, he waved them at me and I felt a kiss on my cheek. I put my hands up to my cheek and found a tiny red stone shaped like puckered lips stuck on it. I peeled it off and held it in my hands. Now I had a kiss from Reddaddy that would last forever and ever.

Thirteen

The day after the picnic, so many things were happening it was like trying to read all the fairy tales in one morning. Mother and Daddy were off at the hospital, trying to get Reddaddy back home, but I already knew he had gone on up to heaven, and Old Thomas was staying close to the big house in case someone needed him. Mammyrosy sniffed a lot as she rubbed her towel over her eyes while she baked up buttermilk biscuits and corn soufflé to take to Reddaddy in the hospital.

It was still hot, and since there was nothing to do and nobody cared, Robertelee and I took a ride down to the pond. We parked our bikes near the main horse barn and sat there for a while, looking at the brown cattails. Since no one was around to stop us, we decided to go down to B-Budd's house. We took the route that passed T-Royal's special pasture, keeping ourselves hidden under the giant oaks, but when we got there, I saw T-Royal was gone. No bull anywhere, not even the smell of him. I knew right away T-Royal had escaped. That's what I whispered to Robertelee.

"Wow-wee," he said.

"Come on. We need to go get Mr. Hugh."

Now we had the perfect excuse to run down to B-Budd's house, so we stopped worrying about being seen. When we reached his place, Mr. Hugh's face was red and he was breathing hard, and when he saw us he wheezed, "Seen B-Budd?"

We shook our heads. "He ain't at the pond," Robertelee said.

"That boy is still sick," Mr. Hugh said. "The snake venom ain't finished yet."

I hurried to tell him about T-Royal, but it turned out he already knew and some of the farmhands were out for T-Royal. Sheriff Ferget was on his way, too, Mr. Hugh said, and then we heard the siren, getting closer and closer. When the sheriff pulled in to the gate and saw us standing there like lost dogs, he ordered us to get in the car and stay there.

"Where's B-Budd, Mr. Hugh?" the sheriff asked. I'd never seen him look so mad.

"That boy's supposed to be in bed," I heard Mr. Hugh telling the sheriff. "But he's done disappeared. His mother is out in the back, fooling with the laundry. I've been trying to find out what happened to T-Royal; he ain't in his pasture, and the fence ain't broken. I'm afraid B-Budd's gone peculiar again."

Sheriff Ferget jumped in the car. I wondered if he remembered we were sitting there as he picked up his radiophone and called his deputies. He didn't say a word to us, but the minute he was done with that call, he turned on the red light and we took off.

Right behind us was Mr. Hugh in his truck. At the edge of the farm we turned down Stout Road, but we hadn't gotten too far when we saw, up ahead in the distance, B-Budd, naked as a jaybird, covered in white milk and sticky honey, walking slowly forward with his shotgun jammed up under his arm. T-Royal Rupert was walking right next to him, rolling from side to side, and T-Royal and that shotgun were covered in milk and honey, too. The bull seemed to be enjoying the adventure even if the flies were stuck in the honey, making dots all over his rump, and B-Budd's eyes were glazed over like doughnuts. As we got closer, I could hear he was shouting out the Twenty-Third Psalm—he seemed to resort to that one whenever he did something odd. He skin was white as an angel's gown and made him look eerie, but I'd never seen a naked person, and I figured a lot of other people must not have either, because cars kept pulling over to the side of the road and the passengers and drivers leaned out to stare.

"Lead me beside the still pastures," he chanted. "Lead me in the paths of righteousness for His namesake." He turned to T-Royal and began to cry out, even louder, "Moses never saw the land of milk and honey, and here we are at it!" and T-Royal mooed while swarms of bees buzzed around them as if they had found something. B-Budd and T-Royal looked completely content.

There was never traffic out on Stout Road, but now a traffic jam began to form, and nobody seemed to know what to do, not even Sheriff Ferget, who kept calling in over his radio to his deputies.

Mr. Hugh drove up near to where B-Budd was. He pulled over and got out of his truck. He was carrying a halter, and he quietly approached B-Budd from behind. When he was close, he aimed to put a halter over T-Royal's head, but the bull yanked his head to the side and, with his polled horns, punched Mr. Hugh in the stomach. I could see from Mr. Hugh's face he was badly hurt, and I couldn't imagine why T-Royal had done that. He loved that bull completely, and I'm sure he thought that bull loved him. He pressed one hand to his stomach, and I saw he was trying to stop the blood. With his other hand he threw a shirt over B-Budd, and just as he did, the deputies pulled up and raced over to help, and as they grabbed him and moved him over toward the truck, I just sat there staring.

One of the men grabbed the halter leash and led T-Royal back toward the farm, and Sheriff Ferget turned around and began to drive back to the farm. He still hadn't said a word to us. I didn't know what was going to happen to B-Budd, but I was pretty sure I wasn't going to see him again anytime soon. When Sheriff Ferget dropped us back at the house, I knew better than to ask anything. He seemed like he had his hands full.

So Robertelee and I just ate dinner that night without asking anyone any more questions, and we didn't say a word—not even to each other—about the strange thing we'd seen. I couldn't stop thinking about B-Budd and Reddaddy all night long, and early the next morning Daddy and Mother came home. I heard them walking downstairs, so I sneaked into their room, and I saw Reddaddy's suitcases on the floor of their bedroom. Relief flooded my body. I skipped out of there and down the hall calling out, "Reddaddy's home."

Daddy came up and put his hand on my shoulder. "Missy," he said solemnly, "Reddaddy won't be coming home. His heart just gave out. He's died, Missy."

At breakfast everyone was quiet except Mother. She kept saying over and over, "He shouldn't have eaten the barbecue. He shouldn't have been dancing the boogie-woogie. He just shouldn't have . . . He shouldn't have run up and down those hills. . . ."

Daddy looked sad, but he shook his head at Mother. "Lucy, he'd have given his life for Old Thomas and the kids. Maybe he did. . . ."

I tried not to think about that. I had so many questions I wanted to ask, but right after breakfast Mother got on the telephone and stayed there most of the morning. She talked to me only by waving her hands to get me out of her room, and then she told me I was to be shipped off to my cousin Mary Louise's house for the day. I knew I couldn't argue with her, but I didn't want to go. Mary Louise always wore pink shoes, and she had a nurse, a chauffeur, and a maid named Maybelle who was so fat she had to turn around to use her other arm. The only good thing was, Maybelle made the best crème brûlée. And Mary Louise also had a much bigger dollhouse than mine. But still I didn't want to go, and finally I convinced Mother to let me stay home.

But Mother pressed the phone against her face and whispered, "Go put on your blue dress with the big lace collar; there's going to be lots of company."

I hated that lace collar, but Mother insisted. Reddaddy's friends and the office people were coming to pay respects before the funeral. I wanted to go to the funeral. I begged Daddy, but he just grinned and said, "Not tonight, Josephine," which was one of those things he always said. "Go on upstairs and get dressed."

While I was changing, I kept hearing the doorbell crying, and after a while I crept down the front stairs as far as I could go without being discovered. In the entrance hall on the inlaid wooden hat table was a bronze statue of Mercury in Peter Pan shoes with arrows in one hand and a hard helmet like half a moon on his head. Men visitors always put their hats on that table or gave them to the butler who was in charge of door opening, but now when I looked I saw so many hats, they were stacked up in towers, and I could hear the room was filling up with people—and I knew there'd be a lot of the same ones who were at the barbecue. I walked on down the stairs and pushed through the swinging door to the butler's pantry and the kitchen, where Mammyrosy was nervously trying to keep order. I know her heart was hurting, because her face looked sadder than I'd ever seen, and she wasn't humming, and she barely noticed me when I walked in. I looked outside and saw that a lot of colored people had gathered around the garage. When I saw Old Thomas, I ran outside to tell him I had seen Reddaddy soaring with the angels. I told him about the red kiss that I'd kept safely hidden in my room, and he smiled and nodded at me like he already knew.

"Why do they have to have a funeral if Reddaddy has already gone?" I asked him, softly so no one else would hear.

"Don't fret, Missy. Reddaddy's earth body is going to be put in a fine silver box in the ground. I'm going to get you a silver box to put your red kiss in. It can stay with you forever because it came from a rainbow in heaven. Reddaddy, who loves his granddaughter, will soon be sitting right up next to the golden throne of Jesus, looking down at us, Missy."

Now I began to notice people were singing and shouting out, "Yes, Lord," and "Glory, hallelujah," so I knew they were praying for Reddaddy. Then suddenly I felt something delicate, like pink butterflies, flittering around my hair.

"What's that?" I asked Old Thomas. He smiled, and he told me that was another sign from Reddaddy, and the others watching around Old Thomas murmured, "Yes, Lord," as they eyed those pink butterflies, which were getting pesky.

"Old Thomas, did I make Reddaddy go away? Mother says I shouldn't have made him dance the boogie-woogie."

"Hush yourself, Missy. She's just upset. Nothing you might ever think up would harm your Reddaddy. He loved nothing better than to boogie-woogie and eat barbecue with his granddaughter. That day when you are called up, you'll find your Reddaddy walking all over God's heaven in those gold shoes."

I kept wondering why saints needed shoes in heaven, but no one ever answered that question for me. It was just one of a lot of questions I was beginning to ask, silently.

A few weeks later B-Budd finally got out of the hospital, and the other questions I had were about him. I overheard Daddy telling Mammyrosy that B-Budd's mind was fragile, but I couldn't ask any questions. I had to eavesdrop on conversations to find out what I wanted to know. Daddy said B-Budd was trying to learn to walk again, but his hands and his head would start shaking and he'd have to sit down and find his tongue. He was shouting out the complete psalms all the time, now, going through them in order, 1 through 150, and his family couldn't sleep at all because he never stopped.

Finally Daddy told me about it. He said B-Budd was wasting away because he wouldn't even eat. His mouth was too busy always moving with those words. Pastors from the lead Holy Roller church down in Mississippi came across the border to pray for him, he said. They tried to extort the devil out of him by lifting him up with their arms and putting snakes all over him. I tried to imagine what that looked like, and I could almost see, but Daddy said the snakes were so horrified they leaped off, and Mr. Hugh had to run around the house with a pitchfork, trying to get them back in the cages.

I don't remember how I learned that Daddy told Mr. Hugh to look for another job. I must have overheard him telling Mother. And even all the way back then, I knew something awful might happen. When men get desperate, they do strange things. Sometimes they shoot themselves, or run away, or go back on their vows, and sometimes they let down their defenses and admit to things that they wouldn't have admitted to a few moments before. That's all I can think of to explain Mr. Hugh's strange change after the day the Holy Rolys left.

In the early morning, Mr. Hugh went down to the tractor shed, where Old Thomas was working on the tractors and talking to Jesus. I was there, too, sitting on the tractor seat, pretending to drive, and when Mr. Hugh walked in, we didn't notice him until he cleared his throat. We both looked up.

"Mr. Thomas," he said, "I'm really grieved by Mr. Red's death. He gave me the only possibility I ever had in my life, and I know I ain't behaved good before him. I ain't been too friendly to you. My son ain't been too friendly to you. I'm askin' pardon for our sins." He didn't stop his sentences or slow down near the end; he just kept talking and talking, almost as if no one was there to listen.

"My boy is in terrible shape—some poison's gotten into his nervous system, maybe when he was snakebit, and it's been chewing on his mind. My wife and I can't sleep at nights, for my boy is writhing on the floor and yelling those Bible verses, and we don't know what he's going to do. Other midnight I caught him out in his underpants in forty-degree weather, chopping the heads off my chickens. He brought in the thirty-six heads and left the bodies sitting out there on the ground for the raccoons to take away."

I took my cue from Old Thomas, and I just sat as quietly as he was sitting, just listening closely, not interrupting, because it was obvious Mr. Hugh had a lot more to say. So we just let him go on talking about how Sheriff Ferget wanted to lock him up because of all the dead animals lying around, and how the sheriff knew he had joined up with the Klan from across the Mississippi but how now he was done with that. Finished, he said.

"Can't say my thoughts done changed, but I gotta do something else so I can save my son. My preacher tells me my son's demons are punishment for what I've been up to. I can't keep living this way."

Now Old Thomas began to fiddle with a couple of tools, but I could see he was listening closely. Still, he didn't look Mr. Hugh in the face, and I didn't move. I'm not sure Mr. Hugh even knew I was there.

"I know you've got some secret tree out in the north back pasture. The children talk about its secrets, that you do some mighty powerful curing of sick creatures. I beg to ask you if you would come see what you can do for B-Budd. I know no one knows your tree, but can you bring something from it that might make B-Budd normal?"

Old Thomas began to hum, taking all this in with the slowness that in the past would have made Mr. Hugh mad. But finally he looked Mr. Hugh straight in the eye and he asked, "Will you allows me to see Master B-Budd?"

Mr. Hugh nodded, and I jumped out of the seat, and Old Thomas grabbed my hand—he wasn't going to leave me behind. So the three of us walked from the shed all the way down to the front of the farm.

When we got close I could see Mrs. Hugh was out in the yard, hanging up freshly laundered clothes, and perched on the line was a pair of strange birds, something like the airmail birds but in colors like a parrot's. As we got close, those birds began to pay close attention to Old Thomas's movements.

"Come on inside," Mr. Hugh said, and we followed him into the house, the screen door banging shut behind us like a prison cell.

B-Budd was shut up in his small room with the linoleum floor and the army cot. Over his bed there was a horrible picture of a burning cross, and another one of the atomic bomb that blew up Japan in the war.

I couldn't believe what I saw. B-Budd was wet as a dewed lawn at dawn, dressed in a white T-shirt and stretched out on white sheets. I had to think about it to figure out what was B-Budd and what was the bedding. His hands and feet were tied down on some bars rigged around the cot, and his eyes had rolled back into his head so all I could see were the whites. He was reciting the crucifixion psalm, but Old Thomas walked right over to him and bent over and began to shout that psalm along with him. I guessed he was trying to notify the evil spirits that there was someone here who knew as much as they did.

Then B-Budd quickly switched to Revelations, the opening of the seals, and just as fast Old Thomas caught up with him. When he flipped back to Job and rushed ahead to some of the more violent psalms, Old Thomas stayed with him, and I knew there was nothing he could come up with that Old Thomas couldn't recite along with him at any speed.

I kept my eyes on Old Thomas, so I saw him pull a few beechos out of his pocket and rub them in his hands until they were only red dye. Then he pressed those hands into B-Budd's white crew cut, and it immediately turned bright red and smelled like barbecue sauce.

"You evil folks get out of Master B-Budd's hair in the name of my best friend Jesus," he said, and neither Mr. Hugh nor I said one word, because we knew we had to just believe.

Then Old Thomas touched B-Budd's forehead, his heart, his hands. He brushed his black hands across Budd's lily-white feet, leaving a red imprint.

Now, we couldn't know exactly what happened, but all of a sudden B-Budd was quiet, and he closed his eyes, and his body grew limp and relaxed, and after that, without a word, Old Thomas grabbed my hand, turned us around, and walked me out of that room—and we went out the back door, not the front. And as we were passing by the house, I heard Mr. Hugh shouting, "Maw, Maw, come in here! I think our son has been saved. . . ."

II
Changes

Fourteen

~⤙⤚~

In the two years after Reddaddy's death and B-Budd's breakdown, the world in which I had been so special began to crumble like stale cake. Daddy gave up swimming because his china-white skin was too sensitive, he was getting fungus, and was too busy. Besides, without Reddaddy, he had to run the cotton plants alone and also had to keep up with the securities business downtown, so he spent less and less time at the farm. He arrived home only for a quick shower before six o'clock dinner, which Old Thomas served most nights after he was moved up to the big house, where Daddy could keep an eye on his health and Old Thomas could keep an eye on us.

Now that Old Thomas was one of Mother's house servants, she could tell him what to do, and he could no longer sneak away to Bozos or the plant. I bet the sisters were lonely. I liked the idea very much that he was up close, but I didn't say that to Mother, and she invented tasks to keep him busy. To me she was forever saying, "Don't bother Old Thomas. He's got work to do." But like Mammyrosy, he was there when we got up in the morning and there when we finished dinner at night, and that made me happy, and Frightnin' was having the time of his life lounging around the big house anywhere he wanted, sleeping with his drooping jowls and ears spread out like a puddle of melted caramel on the Oriental carpet.

For me, it was a time of rapid change and loss. Seminole, Reddaddy's best horse, was left out in a cold rainstorm, and I saw him die of pneumonia, his legs running against the dirt as if he were galloping in the back pastures with Reddaddy on his back. When he stopped galloping, he was dead, and a smelly truck with a hollering pulley came and hauled him away.

All the Hereford cows got sick with pinkeye, and Daddy had to sell them fast in a cow sale, and even T-Royal Rupert the Forty-Ninth had to go because there wasn't any more work for him. After that, Mr. Hugh was lost. Daddy said Robertelee and I had to stay away from B-Budd's house because he was too weak to play anymore, and then one too hot morning a freak hailstorm with ice big as tennis balls left a heap of damage all over the farm. Mother told me that B-Budd had been left out in his lawn chair and had gotten terribly sick, and next thing I knew, the Hughs packed up their belongings and the chickens, not the rabbits, and moved away across the river to Arkansas, from which they had originally come. I never saw any of them again.

But now that there were no cows in the pastures, there got to be more and more horses—American saddlebreds with long, beautiful manes and tails that had to be kept clean and untangled. Mother wouldn't even let me brush one, so I guessed there was an art to taking care of them. She told me I would spook them and get kicked. She said that's why we hired grooms, and also why we hired Mr. Shorten, a horse trainer from Texas with a good reputation for making champions.

Mr. Shorten was a tall, thin man with long, skinny legs rising up from his jodhpur boots so he looked like a pair of straws stuck into a pickle. He smelled of whiskey and chewed on cigarettes. He had two yellow-brown fingers where his cigarettes burned down to, and he wore a flat straw hat even in winter. He lived all alone in Mr. Hugh's old house and was just as mean a man as Mr. Hugh. He said there wasn't a horse anywhere he trusted. I watched him whipping those horses, and I thought the stingers at Mr. Hugh's house must have felt right at home.

Mother rode only mares, never the stallions, who were apt to throw a fit in the middle of a canter. I loved horses, so I would join Mother out in the stables where Mr. Shorten saddled the mares and Mother gave me her standard lecture on stallions. They were out of the question, she said. No proper lady would ride one. She wanted me to know that in case I got ideas in my head.

Competing in horse shows was supposed to be Mother's favorite thing, but whenever she got up in the saddle of one of her mares to exercise them along the inside walls, up and down the center of the giant barn, she looked nervous to me. Mr. Shorten was seldom pleased by her efforts, but he was wise enough to blame all the errors on the horses. As Mother rode past, he'd crack a whip at a mare's legs, and the poor mare would jump on both hind feet at once like a dog dancing in a circus. After a while, the horse would begin to tremble when Mr. Shorten did nothing more than twirl the whip on the ground.

"Nice ride, Mrs. Lucy. The mare's coming along," he'd say, lighting a second cigarette before he'd even finished the first.

I knew better than to ask questions while we were riding, but after we left the barn, I asked Mother why Mr. Shorten whipped our horses, and she said it was to wake them so they wouldn't stumble. We were in the car, warming up the motor, and she was rerouging her cheeks in the rearview mirror, so I took advantage of the time to try to understand.

"It seems to me that when you get them up in the bridle, the horses are just scared to death," I said.

"Don't be silly, Missy. That's what saddle horses are bred to do."

I wanted to say they looked like they had seen a ghost, but Mother was now concentrating on retwisting her French twist. She had to be neat to walk in the door at home. When she rode, she kept her long, painted-red nails perfect by wearing leather gloves.

I went along with her, but the whole world of saddle horses made me sad. Their tails were broken, and they were tied up in some sort of rig to make them stand up in a curve. They had to sleep standing on all four feet in a complicated brace to keep the tail set up just right. Their hooves were oiled and filed into shape and padded with weights so they no longer seemed like normal horses. Those hooves reminded me of Mother's high-heeled shoes.

Worse, to keep them on their toes as they entered the show ring, trainers jammed a greasy gel called ginger in their bottoms. They couldn't let the stewards see them do it, but I was pretty sure all the big-time trainers did it, because right away it caused a burst of high-stepping. Mother decided I was going to be made into an equestrian. Maybe she figured it was something we could do together that we both liked. Besides, riding was the only thing I could do better than most people my age. I didn't know this at the time, but it also helped the farm's reputation when a young amateur showed tough professional horses. It made those horses look easy to ride so they could be sold at a higher price, though I never liked to think about selling those horses because I was attached to them.

"It's business," Mother explained time and again. "Everything's for sale."

"Even White Socks?" I asked.

"Even White Socks," Mother answered with no hesitation, "if the price is right."

White Socks was the first show pony my parents bought for me. She was a butterball just like me, black with white knee socks marked with black polka dots. Both of us were so round, we looked like two scoops of licorice ice cream. I sat atop her dressed for show in a man's suit with a black top hat and tuxedo bow tie borrowed from Daddy, and people thought we were cute, which is probably why we won so many blue ribbons. White Socks knew how to move in rhythm with the organ music playing over the loudspeakers at the fairgrounds and shows. When the announcer said, "Walk," she walked. "Trot," she trotted. "Canter" or "Reverse," she did those on cue. All I had to do was sit back in the saddle and keep my heels down, and afterward lean down and accept the trophy.

But I got to see White Socks only when we were preparing for another horse show. Three days a week, for an hour each time, I went down to the barn to ride, but otherwise the horse barn was off limits to me. I wasn't allowed to brush or play with White Socks. My parents called her mine, but I knew she wasn't, and I longed for an ordinary horse I could ride through the fields like Reddaddy and I used to ride on Seminole. I would have been happy just being able to stay down at the barn and watch everything going on.

Especially after they hired Mr. Washington.

That was one of those turning points in my life, though of course I didn't know it then. You never know those times until later.

Fifteen

One day after school, just about feeding time, Robertelee and I took our bikes and headed toward the front gate with Frightnin' trailing behind us like reluctant fishing bait. My brother insisted on racing forward, then doing tight circles until I caught up. We were heading to the prohibited horse barn, and I thought we should steal past the barn doors in silence, but he was too busy experimenting with his bike balancing to be really quiet. And then, just as we approached the north end of the barn, a strange dog with hair silver like a mirror and carrying a mousetrap in his mouth appeared at the barn door. He dropped the mousetrap and raced straight at Robertelee. He ran in attack form, eyes squinted and tail pointed straight behind, two branches of silver hair like a pair of chopsticks hanging at right angles from the tail. I was marveling at this strange sight when the dog grabbed hold of Robertelee's gray corduroys, clamped the cuffs in his teeth, and brought Robertelee and his bike to a halt.

"Get away, get away," my brother shouted, shaking like he was like trying to pull his fingers out of a turtle snap, but it didn't help. The dog thought he was either playing or fighting, but the harder Robertelee tried to shake him off, the tougher that dog held on. I was paralyzed. I couldn't think what to do at all. And then, all of a sudden, I heard a strange sound—like someone whistling while drinking a soda—and immediately the dog stopped, let go, picked up the mousetrap, and disappeared back into the barn.

Frightnin', who had just caught up with us, chased after the silver bullet, barking and growling like he meant business but stopping well short of the barn entrance. Robertelee stood up on his bike pedals and got going toward the front gate, picking up speed. I kept up a ladylike pedal, and as I passed the large door I tried to glance inside to see who was in there, but to avoid falling off my bike, I had to keep looking forward.

Robertelee was not happy. He was afraid of what would happen when we passed again on the way back home. He had stopped some distance away and was trying to get his right pants leg back in order. He scowled at me. "Whose dog is that?" he asked.

"Beats me. I've never seen him before. Did you see that silver hair?"

"I hate that dog," Robertelee said. "He's stupid."

"Why's he stupid?" I asked. He didn't seem stupid to me.

Robertelee rode on ahead in stops and starts, trying to look like he could outrun anyone who dared him, turning around to call to me, "I'm gonna ride fast as A. J. Foyt."

"Who's A. J. Foyt?" I asked because I didn't know race car drivers the way Robertelee knew them.

We rode on, but when it was time to get home, we realized we had to pass the barn door; there was no other way. Our plan was to sneak close without making a noise, then zoom past at the last minute.

But I could hear the chain on Robertelee's bicycle clanking, so as we got close I whispered, "Hush, you're rattling too loud." I guessed the dog had messed up the chain on our first run by.

When we got up on a rise, still at a distance, Robertelee stood up on his pedals, put his head down, and sped past the open door. In the same second, as if the silver dog had been waiting in the bushes, out he popped again, taking dead aim at Robertelee's cuffs, this time the other side. Round two again went to the dog, who pulled Robertelee over onto the ground, right into the mud. Clinging to Robertelee's pants and shaking his head back and forth with all his might, he wouldn't let go. Frightnin' ran into the fight, and I was sure I'd have to do something, when all of a sudden, once again, that strange whistle came from the barn and the silver dog detached himself and ran off, his straight tail making giant circles like a revved-up motor. Frightnin' stopped in his tracks and didn't move, and Robertelee got back on the bike. His left side was all mud.

I raced past the door and caught up with him, and, pointing to his ripped corduroys, I said, "We're in trouble now. Mother's going to get you. . . ."

His face furious, my brother said, "It's your fault. You're the one who wanted to come down here," and he took off way ahead of Frightnin' and me.

The next day I realized my brother was getting wiser, because when we left the house he showed me he'd stolen a stack of Mammyrosy's biscuits—the buttered ones she reserved every night for the servants' lunch the next day. He'd stuffed them into both pockets, ready for revenge, and as we set off pedaling, he said, "I hate that dog. I'm gonna get him," and he frowned up his eyebrows.

"If it happens again, it's not my fault, hear?" I said. I figured Mammyrosy would blame me for stealing the biscuits, and I didn't want to take the blame for everything.

Once again the silver dog appeared, quick as a bullet, dropping the mousetrap in his mouth as he got in range of Robertelee, but when he was close, Robertelee tossed the biscuit crumbs into the grass. For a moment the silver dog was diverted; he gulped all those biscuits down in one consideration. By the time he started back on the attack again, we had done a U-turn and were out of range. Only Frightnin' stopped and looked back, tempted to grab a biscuit for himself, but not so much as to do something. Our luck held as we headed on toward the big house.

From that day on, whenever Robertelee forgot the biscuits, the dog would become doubly ferocious, and after repeated counter-attacks, I suggested we try to go in peace. I was surprised my brother agreed, but he did, so we just rode up easy to the big barn door, parked our bikes against it, and walked inside. It was cool inside, and the dirt was freshly spread, and the nutty scent of pulverized pecan shells on the floor blended with the smell of fresh alfalfa. We could hear the horses crunching their feed, and the silver dog, suddenly aware of us, grabbed a mousetrap and started coming at us. But just as quickly he made a U-turn and took off running in the other direction down the length of the barn.

Someone was calling him, but we couldn't see anyone anywhere down there; it was too dark inside. The sunlight filtering in from all the windows didn't fill up all the space with light.

Still, I felt eyes looking at us. I got goose bumps and decided we had best head back home before anything else happened.

Sixteen

~~~~

Indian summer had us in its grip, confusing leaves already worn out of their green and turning to red, orange, wine, and gold. It was Saturday after lunch, and I was in my room, reading movie-star magazines, writing fan letters to Farley Granger and Tony Perkins, but when I heard dogs congregating behind Frightnin', I knew Old Thomas had taken out the garbage and helped Mammyrosy mop the kitchen floor and was beginning his amble down the secret path to the back pasture, so I flew downstairs and out the door. Robertelee was there, too.

Old Thomas was humming, and as we skipped through the tall dead grass, timothy weeds grabbed the hem of my dress and my bobby socks, leaving them pinned with prickly burrs. I figured it was time to find out who that new dog was at the barn, so I asked Old Thomas. But he just kept humming on. "He's a strange dog that carries mousetraps in his mouth and attacks Robertelee on his bicycle," I said.

No answer.

"Old Thomas, you know that new man down at the barn? Is that his dog?"

We'd reached the tree by then, and Old Thomas just shook his head and placed both his hands against the tree to give him support.

127

I thought maybe he had run out of air, but a second later I saw his hands were covered in red ladybugs, each one with two black dots on its back. But they were quiet and paying attention. Old Thomas didn't move until a couple ladybugs got an itch to move on.

"O Lord, the plough is restin' now, all harm to come I see too late."

"You're talking poetry, Old Thomas," I said, and he looked at me and said, "Just ramblin', young'un."

Robertelee and I settled on our regular stumps, and Old Thomas bustled about, feeding and conversing with his strange friends, lifting up a wing, poking a sleeping snake with a stick to awaken him, peeking in the O-holes to see how many were in residence, all the while humming nothing I was familiar with and finally settling on one of the stumps. He breathed deeply and, but for his humming and the insects in the grass, everything was quiet.

"Can I ask a question?" I asked. I wondered if Old Thomas was ignoring us because I had asked too many questions about the dog.

"Ask ahead, young'un."

"Why do we have to eat turnip greens and okra and, worse, broccoli?"

"I sees you hiding dem greens under yo grits and helpin' yoself to only one broccoli bud."

"Daddy says they're good for us, but none of my school friends have to eat 'em."

"Yo daddy is a true Southerner. Turnip greens and okra are here today because their seeds came cross from Africa with my 'cestors. Yes sirree. Jest about the onliest things that came with us was our greens and our religion. 'Cestor Lolani owed his life to turnip greens and okra."

I was sorry it was Old Thomas's ancestors' fault, but I still didn't like eating them. I liked biscuits, and I told Old Thomas so. "Just swab those biscuits in yo greens' juice, and you'll get close to heaven," he said, easing into his stump. "Missy, you's rather be at Bozos, eatin' dem sisters' barbecue, than anywhere north or south."

"That's the truth, Old Thomas."

"Can't rightly say there's better. Miss Lula and Miss Irma keeps a lot of secrets, but the one most secret is how dey gets dem hogs just right. You done seen 'em killing those hogs when winter air comes in."

"Grooooooss," I said, remembering the time Reddaddy took me out there at hog-killing time. "That's where their secret lies," Old Thomas said. "And your Reddaddy and me done got it started."

A couple of rabbits ran past. I pulled my foot out of their way as Old Thomas went on to tell me about the secret of fattening hogs. As he talked, all the animals came closer to listen. The story he told was of Miss Demetra, my great-grandmother, Reddaddy's mama.

"'Cause of circumstances and helping out Miss Demetra," Old Thomas said, "yo Reddaddy and me took up fattening hogs for a livin'. We had no money, but we sure had a whole bunch of broccoli in the yard, 'cause broccoli grew on Miss Demetra's land like nowhere else. And we had jars of bacon grease left over from suppers, so we started feeding our hogs dem things and touched up their feed with some secret juices that came from a whiskey bottle, something Mr. Red and I happened upon in samplin'."

I could see Old Thomas liked this story, and I could see even Robertelee liked hearing it, so we just kept quiet, listening.

"We kept studyin' broccoli, coming up with flower heads so big could use them for boxing gloves. Learnt they came up happiest between blue stones. E'en dem local green snakes took a hankerin' to broccoli patches and laid out in circles with their ends wrapped around bunches. When dey rested there, we knew a storm was coming 'cause broccoli flowers spread over 'em like umbrellas."

I closed my eyes and could see those patches of broccoli. I could always see the stories Old Thomas told.

"Yup, Mr. Red and me brung our first hog growed on bacon grease and broccoli to Miss Demetra, and she passed two days cookin' while we waited, playing harmonicas.

"Miss Demetra got so elevated by de first tastins of that hog, she stuffed up some sausages and toted 'em down to the market. She said dey had Jesus in their juices, said she was gonna sell sausages and straighten out some souls. After dat, wasn't 'nuff hogs in the valley to keep folks happy, and Miss Demetra made a livin' and Mr. Red and me took our broccoli and fatback hogs to county fairs and ne'er had a one left over."

I could see he'd reached a spot where I could ask something, so I asked if the Bozo sisters knew about fattening hogs, and he waved my words away.

"I was jest arriving at that. Miss Lula and Miss Irma's pappy caught us at a Mississippi hog auction. He loaded up a truck with some of our live hogs and carried them north to Germantown. Decided it was the tenderest and tastiest meat they ever tried. When we moved north, in our days on the railroads, Mr. Red and me done caught up with those sisters and helped them fatten hogs and cook barbecue. We was young'uns then."

"So, do Miss Lula and Miss Irma still stuff their hogs with broccoli?"

"Well"—he dragged out his thinking—"can't says if theys do, can't says if theys don't. But if'n I tells you the truth, Missy, when de broccoli's gone, they feed dose hogs turnip greens simmered for a day or two in fatback. Hogs like it just as good."

I was silent, then, thinking about all that, thinking about pigs eating turnip greens. As far as I was concerned, they could have it, and now I heard Old Thomas's humming had stopped, and Robertelee was fast asleep.

"I'm cold, Old Thomas," I said, and he put his grandfather sweater on my shoulders and gathered up my snoozing brother in his arms.

"We've gotta head back, young'uns. Miss Lucy will be upset with me."

He hurried us back home, and naturally we had turnip greens for supper, and I realized after we were back home I still didn't know who owned that silver dog.

It was a few days after that, a hot day with no breeze, when I walked through the endless pastures cinched by white board fences and lines of oak trees on my way to the barn. The brood mares had their babies in some of those pastures, and yearlings and two-year-olds got into mischief in others. Those horses that weren't in training were turned out for the day in the nearby paddocks, and as I walked toward the barn, I could smell fresh manure and sweaty horses, and then for the first time I saw Mr. Washington, and my air escaped so quickly I almost had to sit down.

The most sky was visible at the south end of the barn, and against it I could see the silhouette of a man leading a rebellious colt inside. The colt reared and kicked and twisted like a metal spring, whinnying in a furor, but I couldn't tell who was the angriest, he leading or he being led. When the horse finally put all fours on the ground, he was almost sitting down on his hindquarters, pulling hard against the lead shank the man held in his hand. I watched as it became a pull-and-tug game, until the silhouette began to laugh.

Then it let out a strange cry—"*Eeeehokaheyatoto*"—and dropped the lead shank onto the dirt floor, and the horse fell back on its rump into a sit. Still laughing, the man turned and strutted off like a bullfighter, and the colt stood up and shook itself. Something red, yellow, and sapphire blue seemed to twirl out of the colt's nostrils and whip itself around the flanks and the rump, before taking off like a firecracker. I couldn't stop staring as the colt calmly changed attitude and began to follow the man as if he were the nicest blade of grass on Earth.

I don't know if Mr. Washington knew I was there, standing all by myself, dressed in my Jodhpur pants and boots, but as he walked toward me, I felt like backing up and running to my bicycle I'd parked outside. Were there electric fingers springing out of his chest? Were they pushing me back or pulling me forward? I couldn't move. When I heard the grooms loading sacks of feed into the feed room outside the barn, relief washed over me. We two weren't alone.

As he came closer, I squinted, trying to make out the features of his face, but he was still a silhouette against the light behind him—he and the horse, together like a metal sculpture, black on black against the glare. I gasped, "Oh," as the young horse, a golden-orange chestnut with a huge white face and white markings up to her knees, came closer. She was the most wondrous horse I'd ever seen.

The horse dropped her head low, closed her long-lashed eyes, and balanced on three legs, the fourth cocked at ease as she stood right in front of me, and without thinking, I asked, "What's her name?"

"Sweet Potato," the man answered in a strong, lilting voice, not at all like Old Thomas's or Mammyrosy's.

I couldn't look at him, but I couldn't stop talking either. "She looked like a bucking bronco," I said, and I'm sure he heard the shivers in my voice.

"She's a spicy one at that. Must have had chili peppers in her breakfast," he said as he rubbed her nose and whispered something into her ear.

I was in awe, and the stillness of the horse amazed me. "She's so sweet now," I said, reaching over and brushing her velvet nose a couple of times. As I did, I accidentally brushed the man's arm and instantly felt something electric.

"Who's she for?" I asked.

"No one yet," he said. He turned and opened the stall door. "She's got to have some serious handling first."

Sweet Potato followed him into the stall, where she immediately put her head down to sniff and shift the hay. The man lowered the tailboard, leaving the stall open. The tailboard would stop her from ambling out, and when he saw the horse was settled, he stretched out a hand to me. "My name is Washington, Missy Sara," he said. I was surprised to hear him use my given name, Sara. Everyone called me Missy. But I put my hand in his and was startled by the rough, dry skin. The skin revealed from beneath his black shirt with the rolled-up sleeves was the color of milk chocolate, with dark black freckles, just like those on a chocolate chip cookie, and I noticed he smelled like hickory wood and honey. It also seemed like he was young—not that many years more than a teenager, like I was by then.

Mr. Washington held my hand firm. I didn't know where he lived or where he came from. Questions bombarded my mind. Did he live in the barn? Upstairs in the hayloft was an empty room Robertelee and I had used once as a hiding place, but before I could ask any questions, Mr. Washington said, "Mr. Shorten told me you'd be down to ride your pony. She's saddled and ready."

He let go of my hand and walked into a stall at the end of the row, leading White Socks out behind him. I noticed she was very interested in his shirt pocket, nibbling at it even though he kept pushing her nose away, and I wondered what he had hidden there until I saw the pack of Lucky Strike cigarettes.

"Does she eat your cigarettes?" I asked, as he turned White Socks to the side for me to mount.

"If I don't pay attention, she'll steal them faster than an eagle dips."

I wished I could think of more to say, because the most embarrassing moment for me, always, was getting up in the saddle. I had no spring in my mount. I was so heavy that if someone didn't hold down the stirrup on the other side, when I pulled myself up, the saddle would slip down around White Socks's stomach. I knew my face was red, but I had to tell him before I tried.

"I'm not good at this," I said.

He smiled at me. "Before you start, Missy Sara, take a deep breath of air, send it down into your stomach, then push it out." His voice was so calm, all my nerves went away, and although I didn't know if I could believe him, I knew I would try.

And so I did, but weight pulled me down. He was still smiling. "Breathe with your stomach, not your chest," he said, and I tried again, even though I usually tried to hold my stomach in, not fill it with air.

"Now, grab the pommel and the back of the saddle like you mean it," he encouraged me, "like Samson grabbed those columns when he was getting ready to push them down. And think yourself up."

I reached up to the back of the saddle, lifted my leg up high enough to get my foot in the stirrup, and concentrated on an upward direction. And I was lifting up.

It had been a long spell since I had done it. So long, in fact, I had forgotten how lifting up could be useful in all kinds of situations, but when I followed Mr. Washington's instructions, I floated right up to the top of the saddle. He didn't even hold tight the other stirrup, and he didn't seem to think it strange that I could lift up in the air. He just stood back with his arms crossed like he had known all along I could get on White Socks.

I dared not look at him, so I looked down at the saddle, flustered by the miracle and by this man. "I can't believe it," I breathed, and

White Socks sneezed, shook her head, and flicked her tail in both directions. Then she shut her eyes again, and I was so surprised, I forgot to pick up the reins as Mr. Washington checked her bridle and bit.

"Oops, I almost forgot," I said, untangling them and holding them between my right fingers, two hands full. But I knew White Socks wasn't going to do anything anyway. She was in no rush to get to work.

I looked down at him and smiled.

"Thanks. Oh, thanks, Mr. Washington," I said, giving White Socks a kick so she would at least start to walk.

But she flipped her tail in the air.

"Do you want a crop?" Mr. Washington asked.

"Oh, no. White Socks doesn't need anything but a word from her vocabulary," I said, and White Socks and I walked out into the paddock.

As I went through our paces, I noticed Washington's silhouette filling up water buckets. I noticed when he stopped to watch me trying to sit up straight and ride well. White Socks didn't care what I did. She did what she had to do with no problem, but I knew without knowing why that I wanted to impress this stranger.

After we were finished, after I slid down the saddle and kissed White Socks's soft cheek good-bye, I sought out Mr. Washington to thank him, and when I approached I saw that standing beside him now was that silver-gray hairy dog I knew so well.

"That's the dog that attacked Robertelee!" I said without thinking—the words just slipped out.

"I apologize for that," Mr. Washington said, looking hard enough at the dog to make him cower.

"He truly is a beautiful dog," I said. "Is he yours?"

"I'm sure he claims me, don't you, Joseph?" Mr. Washington asked. Joseph wasn't even panting; rather, he was posing. His head was twisted and looking up at Mr. Washington. "Joseph with the Technicolor coat," Mr. Washington added, and I could see how perfect that name was.

"May I pet him?" I asked.

"Give him a little time to know you, Missy Sara. He's new to this place and not too sure if he likes it yet. He'll come to you when he's ready."

I understood that, and I was glad to be patient, but I told Mr. Washington how much Robertelee disliked Joseph. I resolved that next time I came to the barn I would bring some homemade cookies. That would make him like me, I thought, as I walked outside to my bicycle.

When I mounted my bicycle, the seat, which had been right in the sun's eye, burned my rear end, so I had to pedal standing up, and as I rode back to the house, I wondered who this Mr. Washington was. I had noticed one more thing about him. He had scars like long stripes on his arms, and he wore dark glasses. I wondered if he ever took those off. I wondered what his eyes looked like.

Seventeen

All that autumn of my fifteenth year and through the winter, whenever I went out to the barn to ride White Socks and Mr. Washington held that horse for me, I lifted up, and every time I felt happy. One early-spring day when the heat was especially fierce, I walked into the kitchen after riding and wanted to talk to somebody about Mr. Washington. He still seemed mysterious, and nobody had told me anything about him. And there was Mammyrosy, stirring something on the stove. I opened the icebox door to pour some cold water out of Daddy's metal pitcher, and I said, as casually as I could, "There's a new man down at the barn. Name's Mr. Washington . . ."

Mammyrosy turned away from the stove and said, real fast, "I ain't gonna talk about him. No sirree. I don't want nothin' to do with that upstart. Now, get out of dat icebox right now. You losing the cold air."

I closed the icebox, but I said, "He's real good with horses, Mammyrosy. He taught me how to get up on White Socks without pulling off the saddle. I think he's nice."

She stopped looking at me then and turned back to her stove, but she kept talking, fast.

"Lordy be. Nice? That man is up to no good. I been hearin' that horse trainer had brung him here. Uh-huh. Trouble is on our doorstep. Now, Missy, don't you go down to that barn unless you is accompanied. It's no place for young ladies."

For a minute I was too surprised to say another word. Mammyrosy sounded like Mother, and for a minute I wondered if maybe the heat was getting to her. Her hair was up in a hairnet, and she was perspiring pretty awful. "Mammyrosy," I said, sort of pleading, "what in the world could happen? There's lots of grooms working down there."

Then all of a sudden she grabbed one of her church fans with the flat wooden handle she kept nearby and she began to fan herself so fast, it seemed like she was waving the words on that fan in my face: Jesus Saves Sinners. Then she pulled out a chair and sat and looked at me hard and said, "Missy, dat man brings darkness jest when we ain't ready to shut our eyes."

At the mention of that word, I remembered those dark glasses Mr. Washington was always wearing, even in the dark barn, and I wondered how he could see. I thought there must be something wrong with his eyes, so I asked Mammyrosy, but she was busy murmuring like a chorus, and what she was saying wasn't too clear. Something about hypnotizing and exorcizing.

"What do you mean, Mammyrosy? Is there something wrong with Mr. Washington's eyes?"

But Mammyrosy just waved that fan harder and said, "I'll be glad when your mother gets home. She's gonna be all ruffled up when she knows you went down to that barn alone."

"She won't, Mammyrosy. I was supposed to go down there at two o'clock to ride White Socks. Mr. Shorten gets mad if I'm not prompt, but I didn't know he wasn't going to be there." I reached into the cookie jar shaped like a pink pig and grabbed a chocolate brownie, still warm from the oven.

And that gave Mammyrosy a chance to change the subject. "Missy, watch dem cookies, honey; you's supposed to be cutting back." She looked me over with that eye that she used to see what we couldn't see, and she started that murmuring again. "Um, unh. It's coming on, Missy, It's coming that time."

"What time, Mammyrosy? What are you talking about?"

"Dat baby fat is going to fall off you quicker than raw eggs slip. Lord, dis is stifling heat." She worked that fan up and down as fast as hummingbird wings, but I wasn't ready to give up the conversation about Mr. Washington, so I tried again. "Mammyrosy, do you know Mr. Washington?"

She stopped the fan for a minute and looked me right in the eye. "I can't say if I dos, and I can't say if I don'ts. But I ain't studdin' him either way," and the swinging door banged open, and Robertelee came running through the kitchen, aiming his cap pistol at his imaginary friends. When he saw Mammyrosy sitting down, he stopped and laid his head in her lap and asked, "Can I have a Coke?"

Mammyrosy brushed back his wet hair and shook her head. "You know Miz Lucy don't want none of yous drinking Coke. You can have some juice."

But Robertelee turned and smiled up at Mammyrosy and with his sweetest voice said, "Oh, Mammyrosy. I love you. I want a Coke."

"Juice," she said firmly. "And one cookie."

Robertelee stood up, hung his head, and dug his hands deep in the pockets, but I wasn't paying close attention by then. I was thinking how Mr. Washington hid his eyes, and about those slices on his arms, and about lifting up whenever he held White Socks for me, and about how I couldn't stop thinking about him.

Mammyrosy was calmer now, and she turned to me and smiled for the first time since I'd walked into the room.

"Go take your shower, Missy. You has sweated something bad. But leave those boots in the back hall." As I was leaving the room, I heard her mumble, almost too low for me to hear, "Holy saints, preserve us," and I wondered what was worrying her, because back then I didn't know how much Mammyrosy truly understood.

And then suddenly one April day I walked out to the barn and Mr. Shorten told me we were retiring my pony. "Might breed her to see what she comes up with," he said. The news hit me hard. No one had asked me about it. It didn't seem to count to anyone that she was supposedly mine, but I knew if I complained Mother would make it clear I wasn't the one who paid the feed bill. "What's wrong with her?" I asked Mr. Shorten. I wanted to ask him if maybe I could have her baby colt, but I didn't dare.

"Her feet are getting sore; she's foundering, and she's got plenty of age on her. I think it would be considerate if we let her retire and enjoy the sweet weeds of Wild Grass Farm." He smiled then, and he looked over at the stalls. "I want you to start working on Sweet Potato," he said.

I couldn't believe what I'd heard, and I couldn't imagine Mother would let me, but Mr. Shorten assured me they had discussed the matter. "I think it's about time you learn about showing good horses," Mr. Shorten said.

I had my doubts about this new idea. White Socks and I had been a winning pair, but then I looked up and saw Mr. Washington leading Sweet Potato out of her stall, and all my doubts melted away.

Sweet Potato danced around like a ballerina on toe shoes as she came out of her stall, and Mr. Shorten shook his head. "Have to get the hump out of her back," he said, and he mounted her and rode her fast around the indoor track. Mr. Washington and I stood there watching him, not saying a word, and when Mr. Shorten rode back to us and dismounted, he looked at me and said, "Now you're gonna have to get on this mare fast." He turned to Mr. Washington. "Bring her that bench."

I knew I could mount her without the bench, the way Washington had taught me, but for safety's sake, I let Mr. Shorten have his way, and I stepped up on the bench and I don't know who was more nervous, me or Sweet Potato, as I wound the reins around my fingers, climbed up, and crashed into the saddle, lodging my foot in the other stirrup. Right away Sweet Potato was off in a trot.

She was smooth to ride. I could either post or just sit tight and low. But I'd never had that much energy in my hands. It burst through the reins. She held her head up higher than my own, so I started talking to her, quiet things, telling her how I felt, which at that moment was terrified, whispering so she'd know I didn't mean her any harm and hoped she didn't mean me any. I could tell she heard me, and her energy coursed through me.

I noticed Washington standing on the other side of the track, barely visible in his black clothes against the dark wood-paneled walls. He folded his arms and just watched, and even though I couldn't see his eyes, I could feel that gaze.

"Get those elbows down, and your heels, too," Mr. Shorten called. At least today it looked like he wasn't going to work with his whip.

I was practically standing up in the saddle to hold on. I'd never had a light hand, and Sweet Potato didn't have what they called a light mouth—she liked to go where she wanted to go, and I was learning that fast, and even though I knew we had been riding just a few minutes, I already felt as if I'd been on her back for hours. I was aching and afraid, but energized, too, and I wanted it to end, and I didn't want it to either. She was so different from White Socks, who always trotted calmly, in rhythm. This horse jumped from a foxtrot to a rumba in one second, and then back to a foxtrot a second later. There wasn't much space for posting in the saddle.

"Looking good," Mr. Shorten said. I heard the pride in his voice and saw him look over at Mr. Washington and repeat, "Looking good."

Mr. Washington didn't respond, but he didn't take his eyes off me either. I could tell he knew the mare wasn't safe yet. I don't know how I understood, but somehow I did. And then suddenly Mr. Shorten said, "Time to call it quits. Bring her into the middle, and let go of the bit. Loosen the reins. Give her a stroke on her neck or let your right hand hang on her withers—that'll quiet her a bit. She's got to stand still. If she's restless, that counts off points."

I listened hard and tried to follow each direction, and suddenly the ride was over, and it felt like it had gone on forever and ended too soon. When I was back on the ground and Mr. Washington was taking Sweet Potato's reins, Mr. Shorten looked proudly at me and asked, "Well, Missy Sara, how did that feel?"

I thought it over. "I kept losing my stirrup," I said. "I think it needs shortening."

"Gotta learn to use those knees," he said, shaking his head. "You shouldn't even have to have stirrups if you ride that horse with your legs. That's how you tell her what to do. Squeeze those legs."

I nodded. I knew my legs were weaker than wilted lettuce, but one side step by Sweet Potato, and I'd be tossed like a salad. I was glad for the barn and its long passageway—at least she couldn't run away with me that day. But I knew if she was going to be my horse, I'd have to learn some new things.

I followed Mr. Washington and Sweet Potato back to the stall and watched him unsaddle her. My legs were throbbing and my face was flushed, and I noticed Sweet Potato's stomach was heaving in and out as she chewed wildly on the bits, probably trying to spit them out of her mouth. After a few minutes she eased down and started tossing her head, and as she did, Mr. Washington took out his Lucky Strikes and gave her one. A prize.

A few days later when I arrived at the barn for my workout, Mr. Shorten was upset. Mother had fallen off her three-gaited mare. She hadn't broken anything, because she'd landed on her behind, but everything seemed different in the barn. The grooms weren't whistling, and no one was playing music on the radio like they usually did. Someone had raked and wet down the dirt so there was no sign where Mother had landed in the crushed-pecan-shell floor, and, worst of all, it wasn't Mr. Washington who brought out Sweet Potato, it was Ernie, and I could see she was disturbed, because all that energy seemed ready to explode out of her.

"Where's Mr. Washington?" I asked Mr. Shorten.

"He's out in the training ring, breaking a colt," he said as he checked the cinch, the stirrups, and the saddle pad. But he didn't seem to be paying close attention—he was watching the grooms in the bathing area, who were washing down Mother's three-gaited mare. Sweet Potato tossed her head and whinnied and stretched her neck forward, her nostrils opened as wide as her eyes. She looked to me like she wanted to bite someone.

"You sure are a pretty mare," I said softly, rubbing my hand down her silky neck. I was hoping to soothe her, but I knew I had to get down to business and quickly if things were going to work out all right. I quietly gathered up the reins, and first we walked to the north end of the barn, but by the time we reached the end, I realized something had aroused the mares. I looked out the doors of the barn, and I saw out by the swampy edges of the pond a strange-looking horse, so camouflaged by shade and sun rays he looked dappled. It was hard to see where he was in the swamp, but from his teeth hung a long, lifeless green snake with blue stripes, which he playfully tossed up and down. With his extralong mane falling across his eyes, he looked like a rascal.

Sweet Potato whinnied, and I hoped she wouldn't get too quick with her steps; if she did, I'd slide right off the flat saddle. We reversed south and headed back toward Mr. Shorten, who was standing there with that whip in his right hand, his other hand pressed deep into his pocket. His mouth was closed tight on a cigarette. I could tell we were in for a rough morning.

"Forgive me, Sweet Potato," I whispered. "Maybe we can outstep that whipsnapper."

At first we trotted slowly. Her ears were pointed forward, their end tips curved back just slightly; her neck was lifted high like it should be, her nose drawn into her chest. From my viewpoint on her back she looked so neat with that arched neck, those two long, curved muscles, and the mane growing between them. She seemed power and elegance combined, and as we trotted, she lifted her front legs so hard I had difficulty staying in the slippery seat. I bounced, but she somehow remained beneath me, and we made it to the far end of the barn with no trouble. And no whip.

Every time we passed Mr. Shorten, we both tightened up, and that's when I understood we had become a team. I could feel Sweet Potato as much as she could feel me, and together we made a few excellent passes. Lively. Alert. Good sequence. Mr. Shorten kept the whip at his side, as smoke sifted up through his nose.

"Canter," he ordered when I reached the end and turned around again.

"Right," I said to Sweet Potato, and immediately she led with her right front leg. I felt suddenly warm, as if some sort of white light had passed right through me. Sweet Potato slightly turned her head to look, as if the same thing had happened to her, and that's when I was sure Mr. Washington had returned to the barn.

Next we had to trot the high trot—that's what would be required in the show ring—and as Mr. Shorten called out the orders, I sat deep in the saddle and clucked to Sweet Potato as quietly as I could. She was working hard. Sweat seeped around the saddle pad's edge.

And then I heard it. *Crack!* Mr. Shorten burned the whip against her hind legs, twice. *Crack! Crack!*

Sweet Potato skipped around on her back legs and found her order again. It was all I could do to stay balanced, holding on to the reins for dear life, because Sweet Potato had both bits in her teeth. We were holding each other up just through the tension in those reins, and I tried not to burst into tears, though all I could think was how unfair it was. When we could stop at each end to turn around, I think we both felt the relief. We each took a deep breath, and I looked briefly out the big doors at the natural world outside, half dreaming of escape.

When we reached the north end again and I looked outside, the strange horse had disappeared, but I saw dragonflies whirling all over the pond, and I wondered if Sweet Potato could see them, too.

We made four more passes, and Mr. Shorten said nothing. Every time we were in front of him, he snapped that long whip at her hind hocks like a cowboy rounding up stubborn cattle, and although I don't know if the leather actually hit her, I knew she knew what it meant, and neither of us liked it one bit.

When we turned around once more, there stood Mr. Washington in those black glasses, his arms folded across his chest, mouth tightly pressed, and Joseph was standing beside him. He had given his colt over to Ernie to bathe, so now he was just watching us, and I knew he didn't like what was going on.

I couldn't help myself. Tears began to fall from my eyes, but I tried not to let Mr. Shorten see. I wasn't afraid so much as I hated that Sweet Potato was being whipped. I knew if she wanted to, Sweet Potato could run off with me. In the barn, she was contained by the ends, but I wondered what would happen in a show ring with all those lights and music and flags and people. I hated the idea that the only thing that seemed important to Mr. Shorten was that I look good on her and that she appear to be an easy ride. That meant she could be sold for a high price, and now I didn't want to lose her. I thought she and I might win a lot of championships together. I thought if I could convince Mother of that, she might let me keep her.

"That's enough," Mr. Shorten finally called out.

We stopped in a park position, her legs spread out good. Her sides were heaving, and her nostrils were flared so wide the red veins inside them were visible. She gasped when she tried to swallow, and as I quickly dismounted, I refused to look at Mr. Shorten.

"Poor Sweet Potato," I said, rubbing her nose so that my hand was filled with sticky foam. She juggled the bits in her mouth, and I saw the corners were cut from the force of my pull. Mr. Washington quickly grabbed her and walked her around in circles before he unhooked the snaffle chain and removed her saddle. Then he looked at me and nodded, and I knew he was telling me that everything would be all right. I wished I could follow her into the stall and rub her down, but I knew I wasn't allowed.

Mr. Washington let her have a few sips of water from the bucket, but not too much—too much would make her cramp up—and as I stood in the doorway watching, I wondered if she thought I was an awful person, too, like Mr. Shorten. I decided I would bring her peppermints next time. I wanted her to understand where my sympathies lay.

Eighteen

Robertelee was dramatic about everything, so when he came running into my bedroom, breathless, dirt all over his face and hands, carrying a tiny snake in one hand and two metal British soldiers in the other, I didn't pay much attention.

"Mr. Washington has a house up in the tree. He built himself a house up in the tree—he lives in a tree house in the front pasture. He built it himself. It has a hammock and steps and lots of things."

I was busy reading movie magazines, only half listening, so I turned and said, "I don't believe you. Now take that snake outside before it squiggles out of your hand. Mother will kill you if he gets loose in the house." That had happened before. And Robertelee listened and ran out of the room—who knew where—but the minute he was gone, I knew I had to get down there to see what was going on, so I ran after him, and when I caught up with him at the top of the stairs, I said, "Okay, show me, little brother."

Side by side we leaped down the circular steps to the front hall, racing to see who made it to the hall first and through the kitchen.

Mammyrosy was in the kitchen, preparing eggplant soufflé, my least-favorite dish. I thought it tasted like slugs. But it was my father's favorite, so I knew there was no use complaining and we ran right through, as Mammyrosy called after us, "You ain't up to no mischief, is you?" and we called back, "Of course not."

Frightnin' was stretched out against the back door, so we called to him to come follow us, and he slowly came to life and pushed through the screen door.

I rode my bike at a decent pace so Robertelee and Frightnin' could keep up, and we rode past the pond, where it seemed a red frog or a green snake was resting on every lily pad. I skirted through the picnic area—a shortcut—and dropped my bike on the ground beside the white board fence. We climbed the fence to make our way into the front pasture and slogged on as deep as we could go without getting lost in its jungle of trees and dead vines knitted together to form a canopy above. Thin tree trunks lined up like bars on a jailhouse, and Frightnin' pushed through to the front to lead us through a tangle of fresh green kudzu.

"There, there. Look." Robertelee said. "Two Christmas trees."

I looked up, out of breath, at the sight of two dead trees, their leafless branches jammed into different-colored glass drink bottles. Strange ornaments—little saints and angels—hung from smaller, thinner branches, and stuck in here and there were animal figures made of turquoise and red stones and eagle feathers.

I didn't notice the camouflaged house high up in the tree until suddenly a fur ball of silver fell out of the sky right on top of Frightnin's head, and as the two began to tangle, their growls started up like a tractor engine.

"Stop it!" I shouted, reaching out to grab Frightnin's collar, but the two of them were doing some fierce threatening, baring teeth, and snapping, so I stepped back and said, "Please, don't fight." I understood Joseph was only protecting his territory like any dog would, and Frightnin' had come upon it too fast to stop himself—he was surprised, maybe hurt—but I didn't know what to do until suddenly I heard a loud hand clap from above, and I looked up to see Mr. Washington, who seemed to have emerged from the trunk of an old tree.

"Oh, Mr. Washington," I said shyly, suddenly embarrassed at our intrusion. "We've caused a disturbance."

"Looks like it," he said, but at the sound of his clap the two dogs had sat at attention, quiet, breathing hard. When I looked up again, I noticed the branches spread out like a fan above us. "Is this your home, Mr. Washington?" I asked.

"Now and then," he said. "It's more a refuge for my spirit."

Robertelee was pulling on the rope ladder, eager to explore, ignoring any protocol about breaking into somebody's home. "What a neat tree house!" he said. "Can I go up the ladder and see?"

I tried to shush him, but Mr. Washington was quick to say, "A look-see won't hurt."

"I'll stay down here," I said. I wasn't sure about tackling that ladder, but I also held back because I wasn't sure I wanted to know too much about Mr. Washington's private world. While Robertelee climbed, I sat on the grass, picking clover flowers, tying them into circles. Now and then I sneaked a glance up at the incredible house in the tree.

Thin branches had been tied together with long pine needles to form a dome, and strips of colored fabric were woven in and out of the branches at certain places so that it looked like an upside-down basket. I could see it had taken a lot of work, because if I hadn't been looking right at it, I wouldn't have noticed a platform with guard-rails was completely covered in morning-glory vine and jasmine. What would look to anyone's eye like normal forest confusion was an intricately designed structure.

While I waited I began to wonder what Robertelee and Mr. Washington were doing up there, and I wished I hadn't stayed below. I wondered why Mammyrosy was so nervous about this man, and what kinds of secrets he kept. I noticed the dogs were scratching at fleas—scratching in unison, they seemed to have become a team—and then suddenly I heard a sniffle and a blow, and the trees and brush parted, and, washed in a ray of light, the most unusual horse I had ever seen appeared. It was the horse I had seen by the pond, but now that he was close I could see he was blue and purple and white, as if someone had splattered paint all over his rump and his chest. He had silver-blue eyes and a nose as pink as a rabbit's. Staring at him, I tried to stand, but suddenly I had no power even to move and could only stare at the beautiful creature, which looked me right in the eye. After a few moments, he blew out his nose, turned around, and walked back into the mess of trees, and I sat there in stunned silence for a few minutes until Robertelee and Mr. Washington slid down the rope, fireman-style. My brother's face was red with excitement.

"Wow! He's got cool Indian stuff," he said, but I was embarrassed. I didn't want to bother Mr. Washington any more than we already had.

"We'd better go, Robertelee," I said, but Mr. Washington walked up close to me and brushed a lemon-green grasshopper off my shoulder, and then he put his hand on my arm, lightly but firmly, so I couldn't go anywhere.

"Missy Sara, I trust that you're going to talk to me one of these days soon. You're always turning to leave." He said it softly, and Robertelee had already run off with something in his pocket, so he couldn't hear, but I didn't know what to say.

"Sure" came out of my mouth in a long breath, and then just as fast I looked at Frightnin' and said, "Come on, let's go, boy. Bye, Joseph. I'll see you Monday, Mr. Washington." I figured it was best not to mention the horse, but before I ran, I turned to look once more at Mr. Washington, and I saw he was smiling at me like he seldom did, and I noticed his perfect white teeth, and I realized in that moment his sunglasses were gone, and I could see his eyes, and they were as green as emeralds, like no eyes I had ever seen. And I could feel my heart beginning to dance.

It was just a week later that Mother and I were shopping for my confirmation dress at the Helen Shop, and the same woman who had waited on Mother for years brought out a dress I liked—lime green with frogs embroidered around the hem. Mother shook her head.

"Babies, brides, and confirmation initiates must wear white," she said, and the next dress, white and expensive, was exactly what I didn't like—it looked like a dress for an eight-year-old, not a teenager. "Why does white make me more religious?" I asked.

"It symbolizes purity," Mother said, and I saw she was not going to be swayed by any other color. "You must at least look right. I like this batiste dress with the wide satin sash. Tie a bow in the back, Ruby, can you?"

"Oh, God, Mother," I moaned.

"Watch your language, Missy," Mother said as the saleslady turned her back so as not to be a part of the disagreement.

Not only did I hate the dress, I hated the catechism classes where we had to sit in metal chairs and be exposed to what we were supposed to believe as Episcopalians. The ideas were strange and prompted me to turn my head and look out at the trees. Thinking about them made my brain roll in a kind of shudder, the way it did when I bit into a chunk of butter. We were taught not to chew the communion wafer because it was Jesus's body in our mouths, even though Jesus was long gone—I thought of it as being the same as the way we never saw the cow from which our steaks came. I wondered how many dog wafers Old Thomas had harvested and whether they were the same as the communion wafers.

Our church was an old hay barn donated by a faithful Episcopalian farmer when he died. The haylofts had been removed to allow for a large, open space now filled with long wooden pews. Behind the holy altar was a round stained-glass window of Holy Mother Mary draped in a blue grown, sitting on a rock and holding the baby Jesus wrapped in towels. She was surrounded by rounded trees and fields like the fields on our farm. Suspended from the highest part of the church was a large wooden cross.

On Confirmation Sunday, the church was filled mostly with women in hats decorated with flowers. Mother came with Robertelee, but Daddy wouldn't give up his Sunday-morning tennis game, which didn't bother me, because Daddy never gave up his tennis game for anyone or anything. Besides, I knew he was finished with churchgoing. He said when his mother had died before I was born, the bishop was disrespectful and Daddy never forgave him. After that, he said, he decided he could pray to God just as well from his chair in the den as from a church.

So confirmation and church attendance were Mother's idea, and now I was there, being confirmed, posed before the bishop of

Tennessee, who was dressed in red brocades, standing over us like the judge in the Randolph Scott movie I'd watched just the week before. He was fat, and sweat rolled down his pudgy face as the eight other candidates and I, all dressed in white, pledged allegiance to God.

We recited the catechism in a monotone, as we had learned it, and each of us answered the priestly questions, promising to do on our own those things our godparents had vowed we would do when we were too young to know what we were agreeing to. Then the bishop told us that from that day on we were filled with a Holy Ghost, and when the moment came for him to lay his hands on me—I was last— he recited a prayer.

"Defend, O Lord, your servant Sara with your heavenly grace." He coughed between words, putting his hand up to his mouth. "That he may continue yours forever . . ."

When he forgot the change the "he" to a "she," an even more violent cough made him double over and grope in his pocket for a handkerchief. When he finished his coughing, he adjusted his red and gold–flowered cape and wiped his brow, then closed his eyes to collect himself, and at that moment I looked up and saw right through the bishop. He was transparent. My gaze was drawn to the two giant bouquets of red and pink roses on either side of the altar table, which was blanketed in red frogs and ladybugs. My gaze kept going on through space, past the stained-glass window where the gown of the Holy Mary had turned blood red. Baby Jesus, his feet uncovered, looked right at me, reaching out his hands. I saw the red stains on his feet and thought of Old Thomas's dog wafers.

I quickly closed my eyes and put my head down just in time not to miss out on the laying on of hands. The bishop, composed once more, stood over me and levered his fat hands in the air, moving them slowly toward my hair. Then something like little sparks of electricity stopped him from reaching my scalp, and he repeated the prayer.

"Amen," the congregation chorused, and the bishop tried to remove his hands, to fold them back into the prayer position across his stomach, but my hair had raised straight up and was still attached to his hands, and before we knew what was happening, both the bishop and I began to lift up off the floor, over the choir stalls, drifting over to the hanging cross. Even stranger, the choir, distributed on both sides of the altar, became a choir of colored women dressed in red gowns and singing songs Old Thomas played on the radio. I looked back down from my hovering place to see if Old Thomas and Mammyrosy really were there or if this was a vision again.

I saw them standing in back of the church. Mr. Washington was there, too, off to the side, dressed in black, like the bishop, his arms crossed, his dark glasses on. Mother would have been furious if she had seen them, but she was whispering to my godmother, Aunt Marion, and didn't seem even to notice the bishop and me up in the air.

The music turned into one of our traditional hymns, and the choir turned into the regular choir of white women wearing black and white as the bishop and I coasted back to our places. I heard no applause or gasps, and that's when I knew no one else had seen what I had. I heard the bishop talking about peace, and I noticed I was still on my knees, so I jumped up to join the others.

"The peace of the Lord," he said in his crumbly voice as he held up his shepherd's stick, indicating all should rise.

When I looked down at my batiste dress, I saw three large spots of blood on the hem and felt my mother pull me from the altar and out to the car. She didn't say a word, just shooed me inside and drove home as fast as I had ever seen her drive.

Back home, Mother launched into Daddy, who was sitting behind his newspaper as if it were a protective screen.

"I've had it!" she said. "Her confirmation was a fiasco. Coloreds appeared and hummed in the back of the church, but I don't know how they got there, and Missy paid no attention to the bishop. Her hair got stuck on the bishop's hands, and when he raised his hands up for the blessing, she lifted up off the kneeler. That's when I saw the blood on her dress—she got the curse right there on the altar, in front of everyone. I'll never live that down."

"I bet no one noticed," Daddy said calmly, just peering out from behind his newspaper, but Mother barely took a breath before she launched into a tirade. "I don't know how much longer I can stand these ridiculous religious activities. I've got Mammyrosy lost in trances and Old Thomas humming and attracting every kind of animal known on Earth, and now that new man, Washington, is speaking in tongues to make horses behave. Missy talks like she has had not one iota of education. She's even claiming she sees things no one else sees. I thought we were done with all that once we got rid of Mr. Hugh."

Daddy glanced at me, and we both tried not to grin, but we couldn't help but grin a little. "Spring fever?" Daddy suggested softly, but by then Mother was preoccupied by her French roll—the bobby pins were falling out, and the whole thing was unrolling—and that seemed to be the last straw. It sent her marching up the stairs.

Daddy just smiled at me and told me he supposed I was a grown-up now.

Nineteen

———————

Spring meant dog leaves were blanketing the Lolololo tree, and Old Thomas was particularly eager to pick more and more. He wanted a backup supply of dried wafers, which he stored in the gut of the tree, so now he began to take daily trips, and the day after confirmation, when I saw him walking out to the back pasture, I called to him and ran to catch up. "Isn't it a perfect day, Old Thomas? I'm confirmed. I ate a dog wafer!"

"Yes'm, Missy. You make me proud."

"I didn't make Mother very proud. I got blood on my fancy white dress when I kneeled on it, and the three rocks in my knees were irritating something awful."

Old Thomas shook his head. "Missy, you growing into a fine lady," he said, smiling at me.

"Mother says I have the curse. Do I, Old Thomas? I don't want to be a lady like Mother."

"Jest natural, Missy. Jest God's way of keepin' things going," he said. Old Thomas would never say a word against Mother, and I could see he wanted to steer the conversation in another direction, so I told him I had seen him and Mammyrosy and Mr. Washington in church.

He didn't say a word to that, but his skin had a milky appearance, and he hunched over as if the air had left him, and his humming stopped. I was worried for him.

"Old Thomas, what's happened to your humming?" I asked.

"It's still there, young'un—you just don't hear it so well." He gave me a line smile, not one of his enthusiastic ones.

"Are you all right, Old Thomas?"

Without answering, he reached into the gut of the Lolololo. "Ain't you missing something?" he asked.

"What, Old Thomas?" I looked around, and as I did he pulled out Reddaddy's cane and brushed off the moss and leaves sticking to it.

"It's been here a while, Missy, resting in the tree. Looking kind of forgotten."

I felt my heart sag. I hadn't even missed it, and I couldn't imagine how that could have happened, except that so many new things were occupying my time—riding Sweet Potato and reading movie magazines and Nancy Drew, and trying to understand all the strange things happening around me. "Forgive me, Old Thomas. Please forgive me, cane. Forgive me, Reddaddy. Growing up gets me confused. All the things we used to do don't seem so doable now. Old Thomas, I hope you'll always be around."

His mouth turned down into a frown, and with sadness in his voice he said, "Times is difficult, Missy. Things of the world are alterin' so peculiar that I think Old Thomas is out of style. There's not much place for me no more. I can feel it in my bones. I've been hearin' Gabriel's horn moving up closer."

I didn't want to hear Old Thomas talking this way. I couldn't imagine my life without him. "Stay here," I said. "You'll always be safe here. I need you to fix my soul," I said, and I clutched Reddaddy's cane and felt his memory rushing through me.

"I think yo soul is doing just fine, Missy. You only needs pay attention. Dere's some evil spirits hoverin'."

I thought about this for a while. "Do you mean Mr. Washington?" I asked shyly. "Mammyrosy says he's no good, but he seems good to me. He found me a horse I can ride around the farm. I hate riding in the barn all the time."

"Missy, you betters watch out for dat spring fever. It can get you in trouble."

I didn't know what he meant back then, but before I could ask him to explain, he turned away and walked to the other side of the Lolololo. I couldn't see what he was doing, and a hummingbird with motor wings fluttered near my ear, distracting me. "What's are you putting inside the tree, Old Thomas?" I asked.

"Jest some correspondence," he said.

"Who from?"

"Missy, I ain't sure to tell you young'uns. Some correspondences from a family elder who's been huntin' for me."

As he settled on his stump, Old Thomas pulled out of his coat pocket a sack that smelled like barbecue. He opened it and offered me a rib. "I bet you's forgetting how good barbecue is, now been so long since you got to Bozos," and as he tore off a section of the sugar-browned meat, I noticed his fingernails were square and big, transparent as parlor curtains, and I listened as he began to philosophize about those ribs, and how delicious they were, and how they made everything sensible somehow, and, faster than we should have, we finished every bite.

Stomach filled and the taste of barbecue coating my mouth, I felt a snooze coming on. I looked off over the land, remembering how I used to cross it with Reddaddy on Seminole. The sun hid behind a cloud like a naughty girl behind the white skirt of her nanny, and Old Thomas closed his eyes and began to hum so loudly it became words that made sense, and suddenly I knew things I didn't know how I knew.

"Mr. Washington has been to jail, hasn't he?" I asked.

"He's a regular laborin' man," Old Thomas sang, "but he has secrets. Them Apaches considered him sacred. Found him wandering on a thundering night. Called him Black Sky."

"Did he do something wrong?"

Old Thomas rubbed his head. "He helped out them Apaches. One of their squaws was done wrong. Washington killed a man who done it. A white man."

I took this in and wondered out loud what it would be like to kill someone. I knew that was something I could ask Old Thomas, just like I could ask him anything.

"There's too many folks in jail who found out," he said. "And too many bad accused because they's got black skin. I see de Lord's helping Washington make good now, workin' with his horses. He's done got him a reputation as a fine horse exorcist."

"What's an exorcist?" I asked.

"Men who're able to pull demons out of people jest like Jesus did. Dey says Washington has wrestled devil spirits out of outlaw horses he rode out in Arizona."

"How'd he do that?" I asked, leaning forward, no longer tired.

"Missy, you sure's asking a lot of questions. I guess you done come up in age."

But he didn't seem eager to talk anymore. He kept twisting his hat in his hands and putting it back on his head, and a moment later the airmail birds were resting there.

"Spirits can get in our mouth and speak it when we ain't suspectin'," he said. "Washington owns spirits rising up out of the earth. Ours are more likely to come down from the heavens with the Holy Ghost."

I bet Mr. Washington's green eyes had something to do with his special powers, but I didn't say that out loud. Instead I rested Reddaddy's cane on my stomach and stretched out on my back next to Old Thomas's shaded stump. I looked up at the heavens and watched those clouds change shapes as they ran over each other.

"Things are going to get better," I said. Except for bone cracks coming from Frightnin', who was savoring what was left of the barbecued ribs, the world was still and it felt right, and I knew I was going to fill a dream—I would ride Sweet Potato, and Mr. Washington would be at my side—and as I envisioned that, I felt my warmth wash over my whole body as if I were swaddled in cashmere, and I closed my eyes, letting the sun beam through my lids.

When I opened them, I sensed flames and a light shining so fiercely, I seemed to be caught in a floodlight.

"What's that light, Old Thomas?" I asked, grabbing for his dry hand. I could hear Old Thomas humming, more loudly and deeply than ever.

"Get on your knees, young'un. Lean down low. I think we gonna be delivered."

I was not good at kneeling on hard things, but I would never have ignored Thomas's wishes. I laid the cane beside me and got up on my knees, and as I did I heard a gentle voice from up above calling out, "Thomas, Christ's own, in whom I'm well pleased. I know you. I am the A and the Z, the Beginning and the End."

Old Thomas was humming so fast, I began to feel afraid. He was praising the Lord, and, not knowing what else to do, I joined in until he gripped my hand. The sounds stopped, and I felt suddenly encased in liquid jelly, something supportive, something I recognized from the times I had lifted up and floated down the front stairs at Reddaddy's house, and my knees stopped hurting, my mind forgot thought.

And I just was.

I squeezed open my eyes just a fraction and still held tight to Old Thomas. Through light prisms I could see beside me white and red roses growing out of Reddaddy's cane and Old Thomas's eyes silently weeping with joy, his gold-capped front teeth glimmering.

"Lord, I knows you knows best. Amen," he said.

The sky was a moving kaleidoscope, cubes and triangles of patterns and colors, shifting and inventing. Blue and gold ribbons wrapped themselves loosely around all the animals at the foot of the Lolololo, and those animals panted with contentment, and crocuses sprouted between their paws. A lively stream of water the color of blue diamonds poured from the hollowed center of the tree. One by one the animals sipped from it, and that's when I realized the Lolololo had been transformed into a holy temple with mosaics of precious stones and gold and silver waves undulating across its bark. Seven kinds of fruit and seven kinds of fragrant flowers bloomed on its fat branches, and what seemed like raspberry Kool-Aid dripped from the dog leaves still bunched up in the cross's armpits. Sitting amid all this bountifulness, was Jesus, wrapped in gold and white light, his arms open to receive all that would fit.

He was speaking softly to Old Thomas, and maybe to me as well.

Multicolored sugar crystals, rose petals, giant ice-blue snow-flakes in perfect star shapes, and emerald peas began to rain down upon the spring grass, and I stuck out my tongue to catch a flake, just to make sure it was real.

Old Thomas kept on humming and glorifying, and I shut my eyes again. My knees were in fireworks of pain, and as all the things of the world poured back into my thinking, crowding out the moment, I let go of Old Thomas's hand.

I fell flat on my face.

For a while I didn't remember anything, but when I looked again, everything was back to normal and I saw that Old Thomas was chatting with the airmail birds and blue racer snakes and humming at his normal level. Frightnin' was chewing harder on his rib bone.

I brushed my hand through the grasses to see if the emerald peas were still around, but there was nothing there, and the Lolololo tree was white again, and Reddaddy's cane was brown. I stood up and looked around, searching for something, anything, wondering if this had been just a dream.

Old Thomas kept his eye on me as I brushed over the dog leaves, and that's when I saw it—there, on one of the petals: wet pink stains, miracle marks, Kool-Aid drops.

Twenty

When the spring rains slowed, Mr. Shorten wanted to test Sweet Potato and me outdoors on the quarter-mile track, one step closer to the situation we'd eventually face when we went to show, but out there I couldn't get the right lead or raise her head when I had to stop, and I didn't feel good about any of it, but I knew if I voiced my disappointment to either Mother or Mr. Shorten, that would be the end of that. So I kept working at it, and now, as Mr. Washington led Sweet Potato out to the track, Mr. Shorten and I walked on ahead.

"Now, Missy," he said, "I want you to throw your nerves into your big toe and try to sit back and relax on this mare. She won't get any more nervous than you get."

That's what I was afraid of, but I didn't tell Mr. Shorten. Instead I looked over at Mr. Washington, who was polishing her up, passing a white rag across her glimmering coat, and I smiled because she truly was the most beautiful horse I had ever seen, and I was determined to learn her ways.

That day, Mr. Washington didn't wait around for any mounting magic. When I got my foot in the stirrup, he picked up my other leg at the calf and quickly pushed me up. The mare was not one to stand still very long, and just as quickly I had the reins separated and Sweet Potato skidded off, lifting her front legs as high as her chest. For a while I bounced high, trotted, bounced, trotted some more. Bouncing was supposed to get me deep into the saddle, shove me over her kidneys to make her pick up her front legs, but there was nothing relaxed about it, since both Sweet Potato and I had a death grip on the two bits in her mouth.

"Make her walk, get that head up, no jumping around. You've got to simmer her down. Calm her to a walk. It will count off if she doesn't do a flat walk." Mr. Shorten shouted instructions as I rode in a large circle, Sweet Potato looking at all the sorrel birds on the white fences and up and down the telephone wires. I looked down at the grass and saw a formation of green snakes, their heads popping up. Foam dripped from Sweet Potato's mouth as she chewed on her bits, and I tried to let up, but every time I did, she jumped again. Her ears were back, whether in stress or waiting to hear instructions— whichever it was, she seemed irritated at something.

"Ease into a canter," Mr. Shorten called.

This was not my favorite part. I couldn't feel a horse taking its lead like skilled riders could, and out of the corner of my eye I saw Mr. Washington, right behind Mr. Shorten. Mr. Shorten wasn't paying attention, but Washington was pointing his finger straight at us, and Sweet Potato began to canter, but then she bowed her neck, grabbed the bits in her mouth, and took off, and I had no control. We were at the far end of the ring, with a lot of space between us and the gate, but I couldn't even slow her down, much less stop her. I could only hold on for dear life.

When Joseph began to chase us, Sweet Potato didn't like that at all, and as I zoomed past Mr. Washington, tears in my eyes, he yelled, "Take her down. Don't hold so tight on those reins. Ease up; she won't do anything. . . ."

Ease her up, I thought. I was doing all I could just to stop from falling off as she picked up speed into a gallop and we raced down the long side of the track. I was sure she'd keep on going back to the barn, and who knew the kind of damage that would do to her feet and to me? We were never allowed to gallop on the driveway. I held my breath, and then, in the next second, Mr. Washington was there, standing between the runaway and the exit gate. He took off his sunglasses, and I could see those emerald blazes like lightning bolts coming straight at us. "*Hokaheya, hokaheya,*" he shouted.

Sweet Potato came to such a fast stop, it was all I could do not to fly over her head, though as it was I knew I looked a fool as I landed up on her neck. I quickly regained my seat, but I was afraid to look at anyone.

Then Mr. Washington grabbed the reins and looked up at me with those eyes and said softly, "Come on down. You'll be all right."

I was beyond grateful as I climbed off Sweet Potato. I looked up at him and asked, "What do those words mean? How do the horses know?"

"I'll tell you one day, Missy Sara. But for now, you owe me one," he said, and though he didn't wink, I heard the wink in his voice.

My ecstasy at riding such a beautiful horse was dampened by the fear of her running away, and as I watched Mr. Shorten walking toward us, I whispered to Mr. Washington, "You won't say anything to Mr. Shorten, will you?"

"Peace, Missy. It won't happen again," Mr. Washington said very softly, and he turned and led Sweet Potato back to the barn, whispering in her ear. Her head drooped low, and I could see she was exhausted but soothed by Mr. Washington's presence.

Mr. Shorten was chewing on a cigarette and cursing up a streak, though I didn't think he was cursing about me. Still, I was sure he would find out one way or another that Sweet Potato had gotten away from me, and as I walked into the cool darkness of the barn, I looked at him, my eyebrows raised, but all he said was, "Down here tomorrow, Missy. Ten a.m."

For the rest of the day I felt terrible, embarrassed at being such an awful rider, worried that I had somehow hurt Sweet Potato, aware that no one would tell me if I had.

The summer nights were longer now, and when Mother and Daddy went out for their Friday-night card games at the club, Mammyrosy was our babysitter. That night, as usual, she and Robertelee were deep into the fights on television. I decided it was the best time to get out if I was going to, so I tiptoed into the room and told her I needed a bike ride. "All that fried chicken filled me up so much," I said, "I need some exercise."

Mammyrosy just nodded.

I was wearing green shorts and one of Daddy's big white shirts with sleeves rolled up to the elbow, and the whole farm was in bud, that fresh green that signifies new growth. Mother's daffodils lined the driveway. Until the last one had bloomed, the tractor mower couldn't be used to cut the grass, so it was tall and damp with humidity and filled the air with a sweet scent. The airmail birds must have felt my sadness, for they were flying in circles above me, and as I rode down the drive, four came down to ride on the handlebars.

I followed the driveway and found myself at the barn, and when I got there I realized my eyes were red as beets and my cheeks were sopping wet from tears. As I parked my bike inside the big barn door so no one would know I was there, I inhaled the odor of alfalfa, pecan shells, and manure, the best smell in the world to me—one that came from the earth, not from one of Mother's fancy crystal bottles.

The horses were quiet. As I walked toward Sweet Potato's stall, now and then I could hear them stamp their feet to jar off the flies. When I reached Sweet Potato's cell, the fourth on the right, I saw she was standing up in the straw bedding, her neck hung low, her eyes closed. I figured she was sleeping, and softly I pushed open the stall door and walked in, leaving the door open just a crack. I sat down on the tailboard and wondered if she might wake and come over to sniff me.

She hardly moved, but as I watched, she picked up one leg, then the other, and she moved close enough that I could smell her fragrance. She lightly blew her nose on me, and I knew she was aware that there was something different in her stall. I stood up, moved to her, and began to caress her neck. "I'm so sorry, Sweet Potato. I did awful," I whispered.

She shook her head up and down, and I reached in my pocket and pulled out some peppermint sticks. She grabbed one between her lips and batted it around. "It's not cigarettes," I said, "but baby colts like these. Maybe you will, too," and she bit down and chewed it up.

Then she pushed her nose onto my chest, nibbling with her lips at my shirt and sniffing around to see if I had more. I pulled out another from my shorts pocket and wondered if she would let me reach up and hug her neck. I pressed my hands against her chest, feeling the well-sculpted muscles, slowly moving my hands up toward her neck. When I reached it, I made a circle with my arms, like a wreath, and I held tight to her. She began to drop her head down to lean on my shoulder, where she made herself comfortable. She didn't seem put off by my tears.

"You are such a beautiful horse. I love you so much," I whispered. "I promise I'll do better next time." As the sun set and the darkness in the barn deepened, Sweet Potato's white blaze took on an eerie brightness, and as we stood there, I fell into a kind of trance. I listened to her chew, listened to the swish of her tail, the soft stomp of her back legs kicking off flies. I knew I wasn't allowed to be there, but being there was the most wonderful feeling in the world.

I don't know how long I stood there, though by the time I noticed Joseph standing at my feet, I saw it was completely dark outside.

"Joseph, what are you doing here?" I reached down to pet him, and that's when I first saw a dark figure standing in the doorway. I started, pulled myself away from Sweet Potato, and said, "Mr. Washington . . . Please don't tell anyone I was here. I know I'm not supposed to be. . . ."

Mr. Washington stepped closer. "Yes, you should be here, Missy Sara," he said. "This is your horse, and you love her."

I smiled at him, wondering how long he had been standing there watching me.

"Now," he said, "we're going on an adventure."

"Don't you think it's too dark?" I asked.

"Not dark at all. Don't fear the dark. It's the feminine side of the day. Just you wait."

He reached over and removed Sweet Potato's blanket and tail set and folded it neatly on the tailboard. Then he gently placed a halter over her head.

"Come on, girls," he said as he lifted the tailboard. My heart was pounding with excitement as we walked through the door, Joseph racing the length of the barn and back again and then back and forth one more time.

We headed down to the south end of the barn, out to the fields, where the broodmares and yearlings were quiet for the night. I couldn't believe my eyes when I saw the most enormous full moon rising over the tree line, so bright the night was suddenly as light as midday.

"Where are we going, Mr. Washington? Won't Sweet Potato get hurt going out into a pasture?"

"Not if I can help it," he said.

As we walked, I noticed how strangely Joseph's skin reflected the moonlight, glittering like freshly polished silver, shooting rays of light everywhere. I followed Mr. Washington, who led Sweet Potato, and after a long walk through the tall grass, we reached a flat area where the mares and colts usually bedded down, but they had gotten up and stood there watching us.

"Missy Sara, I want you to get on Sweet Potato," Mr. Washington said.

"I can't," I argued. "I've never ridden bareback in my life. I'll fall off."

"No, you won't, Missy. You just grip with your legs. Trust me."

I couldn't believe what he was saying to me. "I'm too scared," I said.

"First I want you to grab her ear and whisper into it, 'Hokahey, hokahey.'"

"But you didn't tell me what that means."

"It is an old Indian prayer. It means, 'Today is a good day to die.'"

I gasped. "Are we going to die?"

"Not literally," he said, very calmly, so calmly it calmed me. "But we must always be ready for anything that happens. You don't know what might change in a flash. That's a sort of dying in itself."

Sweet Potato had her right eye on me, and as she dipped her head down low, I grabbed onto her silky ear, which was stiff like a starched collar. I whispered, "Hokahey, hokahey."

Mr. Washington leaned close.

"Now grab this lock of mane, the one right at the withers. And ease on up." I knew, as chubby as I was, that was impossible, but as that thought flitted through my brain, Mr. Washington grasped the calf of my leg and quickly lifted me up. I had nothing to hold on to but that thin lock of mane—neither stirrups nor reins—and for a few moments I shivered with insecurity, but then Mr. Washington's warm voice filled the night as he said, "You look fine up there, Missy Sara. You girls are as beautiful as Mother Earth," and as Sweet Potato pawed the earth, I felt myself relax.

"Thank you," I said. She pawed again, and I looked helplessly at Mr. Washington. "She gets so nervous. How am I going to stop her if she runs away?"

"She won't run away. I promise," he said, and he reached and lifted off her halter so her head was free.

"Press your heel into her side," he instructed me. "She'll go easily."

And as I followed his instructions, we began to walk, and I felt her muscles moving in a cadence like a song. My body followed, moving with her, blending together as we walked wherever she wanted to go, forward, calm, easy, following the path of the moonlight.

From a distance away, Mr. Washington called, "I want you to let her trot."

"Let her?" I asked. I had no choice. I had given up all my control, including that of my heart, and, recognizing that, Sweet Potato slipped into a soft trot, smooth as a bedroom slipper. I didn't have to post or try to stay seated. I just moved with her as if we were one. After a while, again with ease, she began to gallop. Nothing could stop us now, I thought, as we rode along in a song of love and surrender. I felt my legs gripping her sides, her skin against my skin, my rump stable, moving with hers and at the same time as controlled as a ballet dancer's. My loafers fell into the grass, and I smiled knowing now even my feet were released, and we joyfully galloped all around the pasture, Joseph running like a glittery moon before us.

The mares, most of them being suckled by their colts and fillies, stood watching us, and as we galloped around and around and around, I felt a sense of peace and rightness envelop me. I have no idea how long we rode—for all I know, we flew above the world on silver strings—but suddenly a low whistle brought Sweet Potato back to where we had started, to Mr. Washington, who wore a huge smile on his face and held the halter in his hands.

Sweet Potato stopped, and I leaned over so I could lie on her neck and wrap my arms as far around her as I could. My feet slid up on her rump so I was almost wholly horizontal, and I knew she was my horse forever. "Do I have to get off?" I whispered.

"No. Stay there," he said, "but we better go back to the barn. It's turning cool."

And in the silence of the night, clouds passing in front of the moon, a railroad whistle in the distance, the crunch of Mr. Washington's feet in the grass, we moved toward the porch light of the big house, which I could see in the distance ahead of us.

"How awful to go home," I said as Mr. Washington opened the gate.

He didn't look at me, but he said, "Don't you worry, Missy Sara, there's more to come."

When we got back to her stall, I slid off as if I had done it a million times and kissed Sweet Potato's nose.

Mr. Washington stood in front of me, his fingers intertwined in the halter, and hesitantly I reached up and gave him a kiss on his cheek. "Thank you for giving me a dream, Mr. Washington," I said.

He grabbed my arm up near my breast, holding me in one hand, Sweet Potato in the other—but it was only a moment, and then he quickly let me go, though I don't think he wanted to. I looked at my arm and saw his fingerprints imprinted where he had squeezed me so hard, and I turned and ran outside to my bike. I knew I had to get home fast. If Mammyrosy asked me anything, I decided I would say I had just been sitting by the fence, looking at the moon, but I didn't know how I was going to explain my missing loafers, which were out there in the pasture somewhere.

Two nights later, just before dinnertime, we were all sitting in the comfortable chairs of the den, waiting for Old Thomas to announce dinner. Sheriff Ferget had stopped by for his weekly visit to the big house.

"You got a mighty strange-looking animal grazing in the front pasture," Sheriff Ferget said. "Looks like something Mr. Red would have liked. Odd colors for a horse. The white gets fluorescent in the night." Mother handed Sheriff Ferget a Coke poured in a glass with a paper napkin wrapped around the base.

"It's some Indian pony that came with Washington," Daddy said. "Says it's an heir of Geronimo's steed. Calls him Indigo. Says he's pretty useful to have standing around those outlaw colts he has to break. You know how animals tranquilize each other. Washington put a chicken in the stall with that Wing Commander colt and a black sheep in with a nervous filly who paces in circles around her stall. Works every time."

I wanted to be part of the conversation, and even though Daddy didn't know, I was aware of a great deal. "Washington says the fillies can get so attached to a sheep that they start whinnying if it gets out of the stall for five minutes," I said.

I wished in the next second I hadn't said anything, because Mother leaned forward toward me and said, "Missy, you don't need to be having any conversations with Mr. Washington. No decent young lady would be carrying on a conversation with a groom."

I shot back at her, "I learn more from Mr. Washington than from Mr. Shorten," and that seemed to suck the air out of the room. Even Daddy glared at me, and Mother looked down, squinting at her needlepoint needle, and said, "I expect you to do what I say, daughter. The barn is not your playhouse."

If I'd been a different type of girl, I might have fallen silent then, but I couldn't, and I said, "Mother, Mr. Washington saved my life!"

"I doubt it, dear," she said, shaking her head, and I realized no one had said a word to her about my runaway ride and it was best for me to keep my mouth shut. I settled back into my chair. "Oh, he just did," I said softly now.

"I doubt it, dear," she said again.

That riled me, and I couldn't help myself.

"You just don't trust anyone black, do you, Mother?" I ranted. I knew she also never believed anything I said. Whenever I told her a horse was loose, she didn't believe me until Mr. Shorten and a couple of farmhands confirmed it. But now, as Daddy shot me a furious look, I lowered myself in my chair and watched Sheriff Ferget take a sip of Coke.

"Watch how you talk to your mother, young lady," Daddy said forcefully.

"And you listen to me, Missy," Mother said. "Mr. Washington may have done miracles with the colt crop, but there's something about him that strikes terror in me." Mother tucked up her French roll and turned to Daddy. "And he's always looking at Missy," she said.

"How do you know who he looks at, Mother? He's always got dark glasses on," I retorted, and that infuriated Daddy. "Up to your room right now, Missy," he said. I stood up. I knew he would always side with Mother, even when she was wrong.

But as I walked out of the room, I wasn't sorry for defending Mr. Washington. I sat down on the green-carpeted circular stairs just a few feet from the den to listen—I wanted to hear anything anyone had to say about Mr. Washington. I especially wanted to know how he could be an Apache Indian if he was black-skinned, and I didn't understand why Mother was afraid of everybody who was colored and nobody who was white. Whenever she moved from one room to the other in our own house, she carried her pocketbook, so I knew she didn't even trust Mammyrosy or Old Thomas, and I couldn't imagine why.

I heard my name—it was Sheriff Ferget who was talking. And I leaned in to try to hear every word. "Shorten said Sweet Potato was good enough that she's sure to take the blue in the amateur stakes class," the sheriff said.

"We hope so," Mother said, "but she takes a death grip on the reins."

"I don't know how Shorten does it," the sheriff went on. "He drinks more coffee than an airline pilot and cigarettes in between. You'd think he'd be a bundle of nerves and conversation, but on those horses, he's calm as peanut butter."

"Shorten has been doing a right decent job building the stable up again," Daddy said. "He knows his pedigrees almost as well as Lucy does, so I'm sure the honors will start coming in once they start on the show circuit, and Shorten swears by Washington, so I think we need to trust his judgment."

I could hear Sheriff Ferget sipping his Coke.

"I agree. He's not going to cause a fuss. He's downright respectful and intelligent," he added. "Are you going to make it up to the Germantown show this year, Mr. Georgelea?"

"I'd like to see Missy's debut on Sweet Potato, but I probably won't be able to get there. Hope she won't be too disappointed."

It didn't surprise me to hear that. Daddy didn't show up for anything I did—not church, not school, not horses. He was always too busy, but I was glad to hear someone was defending Mr. Washington, at least.

"It's going to be a big night for her," the sheriff said. "Quite a step up from White Socks. Everybody'll be watching to see if she's going to follow in her mother's footsteps. You've got a legacy going here."

"I hope it's a good legacy," Mother said, and I could tell her fury had passed.

"Dinner's served, Mr. Georgelea," Old Thomas announced, and as they rose to go eat supper, I ran on up the stairs to my room. I didn't care. I didn't like turnip greens and black-eyed peas anyway. All that mattered was that soon Sweet Potato and I were going to show off all we had learned about each other.

Twenty - One

The week of the horse show, I couldn't sleep at all, and every night I replayed in my mind's eye the night out in the field with Sweet Potato and the vision with Old Thomas. I could feel sides being taken up within my heart.

The day of the show, a dozen times I tried on my riding clothes—a black suit like a man's, with straight jodhpurs and a formal jacket and tie and my derby hat—to see how fat I looked. When I was satisfied, I rode my bike to get out of the big house. The barn was filled with visitors in town for the Germantown Charity Horse Show, but I had orders from Mother and Daddy to stay away—Mother worried I might say something that would discourage a buyer—so I had to ride around, waiting until lunchtime on opening day.

It was a Thursday, and as Mother and I arrived, I saw that the hunter and jumper classes were in progress in a side ring. The official opening was to be that night in the principal ring, so the grounds were a maze of metal trailers and horses in plaid blankets unloading down a ramp. Some were completely covered to their heads, like medieval warhorses with openings only for their eyes and mouths. The show workers were draping the last of the red-white-and-blue bunting around the ring, and jumps had been set up for the first night class. The organist sat off in the corner near the officials' box, practicing her scales. A tractor moved around the ring, watering down the dirt so it wouldn't get too dry. Daytime entries of hunters and jumpers trotted in a practice ring as a lady in the announcer's seat called out numbers that needed to check in at the paddock.

Our set of five large stalls were draped in the Wild Grass Farm's green and white colors—stalls for the five horses we would be showing over three days. Five grooms wrapped the horses' legs in cotton bandages, rubbed their bodies with white rags, and unloaded special feed brought just for our horses. As we walked around, I peeked into Sweet Potato's stall and saw Mr. Washington at work painting grease on her hooves. He must have heard me, because he turned and looked up. "You ready, Missy Sara?" he asked.

"Now I am, thanks to you, Mr. Washington," I said, looking around to make sure Mother wasn't nearby. When I saw she was busy talking to one of the other grooms, I leaned in and said, "I've looked forward to this night more than anything in my life. I love Sweet Potato more than anything in the world." I balanced on the stall board and relaxed into the conversation. "Even Mr. Sharpen seems pleased with my riding now. You're a miracle man, Mr. Washington." I turned my attention to my shining mare. "And Sweet Potato, remember, now, don't you get all feisty when you see the bright lights and people."

Mr. Washington shook his head. "Be at ease, Missy Sara. I'll be ringside. Sweet Potato will listen to my voice. Most important is you ride like you know how to ride. You've been in a show ring plenty of times before; just don't be nervous."

But this was different, and I knew it. "White Socks always took care of me," I said. "She did everything automatically."

"I'll take care of you this time." He rested his arms on his bent legs and looked straight at me. "Remember the moon."

I couldn't possibly have forgotten, and I felt that little heart flutter again as I whispered, "Do you think we have a chance at the blue?"

"Missy Sara, give me your hand," he said, and as he rose from his crouched position, I held out my hand. I followed his as he placed a small white stone frog with turquoise eyes into my palm. He turned it over, and I saw a red speck on its stomach. "This wise-frog fetish was gifted to me by an Anasazi Indian chief I knew well," he said softly. "I've had it a long time. It's yours now. Keep it with you tomorrow night."

I couldn't say a word, I was so moved, and then a line came to me from the weddings I'd gone to: "something old, something new, something borrowed, something blue . . ."

Mr. Washington laughed as that little frog seemed to engrave itself into my palm. For a minute I was sure I saw it glow, and Sweet Potato put down her head and rested her nose in my palm and ever so lightly blew on the frog.

"Now put it in your pocket, Missy Sara," he said. "Don't lose it."

"Oh, no. I won't ever lose it," I said.

"You are the Sacred Virgin of the Moon Frog, Missy Sara," Mr. Washington added in a voice as soft as cat's fur.

I laughed, embarrassed to have such a thing said to me. "I will never forget that night under the moon," I said so quietly I almost couldn't hear my own words. "I hope Sweet Potato won't either."

And for a moment I felt as if I were in that field again, and then I heard Mother's voice right behind me. "What are you doing, young lady?" I quickly closed my hand and pushed the stone frog into my jeans pocket, and the spell was broken.

"Don't bother the grooms while they're working," she said coldly. "There's a lot to be done. Tonight Mr. Shorten rides Denmark's Golden Glory in the open class."

I turned from the stall and looked at Mother and said, "I was just looking in on Sweet Potato."

"Everything all right?" Mother addressed Mr. Washington without so much as a hello.

"Yes, ma'am," he said. "We're all ready to go."

"Mr. Shorten is pleased with Missy's progress on Sweet Potato," Mother said. "I'm told a lot of credit goes to you." I was relieved that Mother had chosen for a moment to express some kindness, but Mr. Washington was quick to say, "Ma'am, it's Missy Sara who has done the work, not me. She deserves the night."

"Yes," Mother said as she wandered off to see how the other horses were faring. A few steps away, she turned and said to me,

"Come on, Missy, we've got to get home. You'll need a good night's sleep tonight." I agreed.

It was Friday when Sweet Potato and I would make our debut. All that day I spent the time in the kitchen, watching Mammyrosy cook and Old Thomas polish the antique silver with a paste that had an odor like floor wax.

"Come on here, Missy. Help me mix this batter," Mammyrosy said. "I guess it's about time you learned some cooking secrets." I knew she was being kind only because I was restless and could not settle down.

Old Thomas seemed tired and kept slipping into a sleep, his white eye opening and closing as if he had no control over it. I wanted so much to show him the frog and ask him what "Sacred Virgin of the Moon Frog" meant, but I knew it wasn't a wise thing to do in front of Mammyrosy, since she had made it clear she didn't want to hear about Mr. Washington.

Mammyrosy measured the butter and flour and sugar by her hands. "Just instincts," she said when I asked her how she knew they were correct. Once everything was in the bowl, she handed me the long wooden spoon, the same one she had been using for as long as I had been around, and I stirred until my arm muscles gave out.

"Get them air bubbles out, Missy. Is you done already?" she asked, wiping her hands on her towel and taking over the wooden spoon.

"Mammyrosy, I'm not strong like you."

She laughed very lightly and pinched my arms where the muscles should be. "Lordy, Missy, you need to lift some logs," she said. "What kinda cook you gonna make? Bless my soul."

"Well, you better get to teaching me. Who knows, I might get married any day." I dipped my finger into the sweet-tasting batter.

"Get your fingers out of that," she said firmly. "This ain't for eatin'. It's for cookin'." Mammyrosy didn't believe in finger or bowl licking.

"Call me when the cake is done," I said. "I'm going to my room to listen to records." I wanted to peek at my frog again, and think about it.

In my room I put five 45 records on the player and crawled into my canopied bed to rest. All my clothes for the horse show were laid out on the chaise lounge. Bill Haley & His Comets flipped down, singing "Rock Around the Clock." I turned it off. Suddenly I didn't want to listen to anything so bouncy. I looked out the window and through the giant magnolia trees to see if I could see the Lolololo tree, but it was invisible, and I wished I could take a trip out there to calm my nerves, but I knew I had to stay in the house until Mother came home from the ring. If I was gone when she arrived, I'd never hear the end of it.

She finally returned around four o'clock and called me into her bedroom. When I walked in, she had already changed into her red satin robe and was piling her hair atop her head, preparing to take a bath.

"Missy, I have some disappointing news. I know it's going to break your heart, but there's nothing I can do about it," she said.

My heart stopped, and for a moment I worried that they had fired Mr. Washington. Or maybe Sweet Potato had fallen ill. I held my breath as Mother rubbed thick white cleansing cream into her face.

"You cannot ride Sweet Potato in the show tonight," she said.

"What?" I gasped. "Why not? Why can't I ride her?"

Mother's voice was firm and unsympathetic, and she looked like a witch to me with her white face and her hair wrapped atop her head as she explained they had sold Sweet Potato that very afternoon. "For a very high price," she said, "to one of the top stables in the country." She said they had been so impressed by Sweet Potato, and by Mr. Shorten's description of her, that they had flown right down from up north and bought her for cash. "I couldn't turn it down," she said.

"You're taking her away from me? You've sold her out from under me? How could you do this, Mother? She's my horse." I could feel my soul breaking to pieces.

"There's nothing I can do about it now," Mother said coolly as she stood and walked to her boudoir, where she pulled out a pair of silk stockings.

"After all the work, you have to let me ride her once," I wailed. I was so hurt I didn't know if I was angry or simply sad, but I knew one thing. I would never ever trust Mother again.

"We can't risk something happening to her, Missy. We've already signed the papers."For a moment we both were silent, and then I began to yell. "I hope all your stockings have runs in them. I hate you! You are the cruelest person I've ever known—you used me to sell your damn horse!"

Mother turned and raised her hand to slap my cheek, but before she could, I looked straight at her. "Don't you use that language with me, young lady," she said.

"Well, Daddy says 'damn,'" I said. She couldn't hurt me with a mere slap. She'd already hurt me far worse.

"That's no excuse," she said, pulling her hand back and turning to look into her vanity mirror on the dressing table.

"Money. The only thing that matters to you is how much something costs. You don't even care if you break someone's heart." I ran out of her room, down the curving stairs, and through the kitchen, where neither Mammyrosy nor Thomas so much as looked up. I leaped over Frightnin', who was lying against the back door, waiting for Daddy, and I ran outside to wherever I could get. My insides were on fire with fury, and all I could think about was how much I hated Mother for deceiving me and breaking my heart.

I kept running, and when I was deep in the back pasture, I felt someone following me. I wasn't sure if I should turn back to look or just run faster, but when my curiosity got the better of me, I turned and saw Joseph on my heels.

I kept going until I reached the Lolololo tree, and this time it didn't hide itself with clouds or mist. I hurled myself into its thick trunks where all the O-holes were, and I wept until there was no more water in me. I felt the tree bend over to embrace me, surrounding me with its loving spirit, and there I knew I was safe and cared for.

"How could they do this to me? How could they?" I cried to all my animal friends and to the tree. I reached into my pocket and pulled out the white frog with the turquoise eyes and rubbed my fingers across its belly. I wondered if Mr. Washington had given it to me because he'd known something was going to happen, because he'd known I would need strength. And suddenly the white frog moved, and I heard a voice saying, "It's not important, Missy. It's not the end of the world. You will do greater things than this. Don't wrench your heart. God loves you more than this."

"*Hokahey*," I whispered. "It really is a good day to die. I hate this world." I looked up and over my shoulder, but I saw no one but a new family of raccoons standing nearby and a red fox on a long, old branch. Airmail birds rested on other branches, and green snakes and blue racers peeped their heads out of the holes. I saw some foreigners, too—red frogs that had crawled into spaces not occupied by the airmail birds. I thought the ladybugs must be confused by all those frogs occupying their favorite spots.

I swallowed and wiped my eyes and looked at all of them. "I know you're my friends," I said. "Just like Old Thomas. But why are most humans so mean? Why did my own mother do this to me?"

The minute I said this, a quilt of pink and yellow butterflies landed in my hair, on my nose, and on my arms. For a minute, their wings tickled, and despite the tears, I giggled. I looked at them, and I couldn't help but smile. "I believe in you and in the Lolololo tree, but it's too hard to believe in anything else."

When I noticed Joseph hadn't left my side, I introduced him to the tree and to its occupants, and I thanked them for allowing me to come here without Old Thomas as my guide. Joseph didn't move. He simply sat and watched as if he were a curious tourist, and I must have fallen asleep, because when I finally stirred, it was dark outside and the moon was bigger than a silver dollar against the black sky.

Joseph licked my arm, and I realized he had accepted me at last, and I knew I wouldn't return to the big house until I was sure Mother had gone. Let them worry about me.

But as the air grew cool, my courage wavered. I was wearing only a T-shirt and shorts, and I began to tremble and decided I had better walk home. I hadn't gone far down the path the green snakes laid out for me when I saw Indio standing in my way. A big cardboard note was tied to his halter, and I reached out and tipped it toward the moon so I could read the words.

"To the Sacred Virgin of the Moon Frog. I am yours to run as fast as the wind and to dream until there is no more to dream, to paint the world with your heart of gold, and to go where no other would go. You need fight no more."

I reached out and wrapped my arms around Indio's neck and cried again, and I felt his chin press against my shoulder. And then somehow, with no effort, I was up on his bare back, with only his mane to hold on to, and he took off across the pasture. I wondered if we were flying toward the Milky Way, and I wasn't the least bit afraid.

Twenty - Two

I don't remember that night or the next day because of what happened on Saturday night. I was in my room, listening to music,
when I heard Frightnin's howl—a howl so eerie, I knew something
terrible must be happening. I jumped out of bed and ran down the
back stairs, and as I came around the corner, I saw Old Thomas lying
there on the speckled linoleum of the back hall. Just a few hours
earlier he had served us scrambled eggs and bacon and pompadour
pudding—custard and chocolate sponge, one of Daddy's favorites.
Mammyrosy had washed and put away all the dishes and walked
down to her house, but Old Thomas had stayed to finish up cleaning and to empty the garbage. He had done all that. And he had fed
Frightnin'; I saw his food still in his bowl. But he had not yet taken
off his starched white serving jacket—it was clean as a new tool—
and I knew right away Old Thomas was dead.

There was no blood. No one had heard a cry of pain. Both his
white eye and his good eye were wide open, aimed straight up at
God, and he lay almost at attention, not a curl in his body. I leaned
down to his almost-bald head and rubbed it, and I kissed his forehead right in the center and felt his skin as cold as ice cream. "Thank
you, wonderful friend," I whispered. "Thank you for your life."

Then I stood up and shouted for Daddy, and a moment later I

heard my father's elegant shoes tapping down the long, L-shaped back hall. Old Thomas had fallen in the short L part, right at the back door where Frightnin' usually kept vigil. Mother's high heels followed Daddy's brogues, and after that came what sounded like a thousand little toenails of Mother's new dachshund puppies.

It's funny the things we remember in those big moments in life. I remember Mother was dressed in a floral-print dress with a matching jacket—she was to present the trophy in the three-year-old stakes class at the Horse Show. It was championship night.

I looked outside and saw the dusk wind blowing tenderly, wiping away the day's mugginess. The late sun was unusually bright for summer, clarifying the tree and shrub shapes so there was no doubt about them. The wind chime I had given Mother for Christmas was making cathedral sounds, and Frightnin' continued his off-key howl until finally Daddy reached out to calm him.

Daddy said nothing. He bent down and put his fingers on Old Thomas's neck, and he knew right away his life was finished. "Old Thomas has gone. God bless his soul," Daddy said, and he pressed Old Thomas's eyelids down so he wasn't looking anymore. Then Daddy looked up toward the heavens. "Well, Father, your friend is ready to join you," he said.

Mother mumbled, "What a place to die," and I could see my father draw up in anger, but Mother quickly shut up, and Frightnin' laid his head on Old Thomas's leg.

"Poor Old Thomas," I wept. "I love him more than anybody in the world. What do we do now, Daddy?"

"First, we must get this dead body out of the back hall," Mother said, but neither Daddy nor I paid her any attention. When her puppies gathered around to sniff Old Thomas's body, Frightnin' growled fiercely and warned them this was his territory, and Mother fanned her hands back and forth, shooing them away. She turned to leave through the kitchen, and as she passed through, she stopped at the cookie jar and reached in for a handful for her yapping dogs.

"Get a sheet, Lucy," Daddy said.

Without turning around she said, "You take care of it, Georgelea. Here comes Marion to pick me up for the horse show. It's stakes night." And we all looked up and saw through the window the powder-blue Cadillac pulling up the drive.

"I'll get the sheet, Daddy," I said, and I stood for a moment over Old Thomas and hummed, "*Hokahey.*" Then I hurried upstairs to get one of Mother's expensive Leron sheets.

When I came back downstairs, I laid the sheet over Old Thomas and listened as Daddy spoke on the phone to the sheriff. The evening sun rays shot through the west-facing kitchen window, and I could have sworn they stopped at Old Thomas's heart. The rays were thin, straight bars, and I saw tiny angels no bigger than my fingers running up and down those bars, carrying bundles wrapped in white. A mass of pink butterflies appeared and, wings flapping in a final blessing, circled Old Thomas. I knew Old Thomas was being accompanied, that he might already have woken up to meet his friend Jesus, might already have shaken his hand and been kissed by a thousand angels. He surely had already seen Reddaddy. I could feel it in my soul.

When the ambulance nurses and Sheriff Ferget arrived, Frightnin' was once again blocking the back entrance, once more asleep, and no matter how hard we tried, we couldn't get him to move, so everyone had to step over him to get to the body Old Thomas had left behind, and I knew even then Frightnin' wasn't going to stay around forever either—not without his best friend.

When they finally did lift him off the floor and over Frightnin' and out the back door, I saw the floor was covered in dog leaves that left Old Thomas's impression on the linoleum. Quickly I gathered them up and put them in a paper cup, and I wondered if I ought to take them to the sisters at Bozos. I was sure they would know what to do with them.

To attend Old Thomas's funeral, Mother and I were decked out in proper hats, gloves, girdles, stockings, and Sunday clothes that covered the knees, and Daddy had given up his regular tennis game. When we walked into the church, the elders thanked us in front of everyone, including the dozens of oversize colored women in black hair bobs and long white robes who took up the entire front half of the old wooden church—the choir. The preacher said we were special friends to Old Thomas his whole life and did good things for him. I blushed because he'd picked us out of all the people there—all those friends of Old Thomas I had never seen. The church was full to the brim, and our family and Sheriff Ferget were the only white people there.

Mother leaned over me and whispered to Daddy, "They just want you to give a big donation to the church." She adjusted her hat of red cherries with leaves. "We do that for the servants," she told me.

"Hush up, Lucille," Daddy said.

I'd overheard Mother that morning fretting on the phone with Aunt Marion about finding help with the same loyalty as Old Thomas. "Colored people are getting so impertinent," she said, and I ran out of the room because I didn't want to hear any more. I didn't see the world the way Mother saw it, and by then I was beginning to understand I never would.

The preacher motioned the congregation to proceed toward the front, where a thick bronze coffin trimmed in gold lace and silver satin—the very thing Old Thomas had requested for a bona fide rejoicing funeral—sat opened like a box of Whitman's chocolates. All I could think about was how much I wouldn't want to lie in one of those metal boxes, but I remembered Old Thomas once explained to me that the Lord didn't want our bodies. "Just our souls," he said. "We put our bodies in boxes, but the good souls of the Lord's chosen soar right on up through the pearly gates." I always thought about that when I looked at the tiny silver box with the red heart in it that Old Thomas had given me when Reddaddy died. And I thought about it again now.

To do right by Old Thomas, we all had to walk down the aisle and pass by the coffin to pay respects, and as I walked past I wondered if he knew we were doing this. I thought he probably wouldn't like all the folks looking at him asleep in that box.

"Don't make me look," Robertelee cried to Mother as she tried to pull him out of the pew to join the parade.

"Stay with Mammyrosy, then." She patted his head. "We'll be right back."

When I stood up, I turned and saw Mr. Washington in his dark glasses, standing in the back with a number of other young men, and I was glad he was there, but then, suddenly, as I walked along the white carpet, I began to cry, and it wasn't just tears falling. I sobbed with great hiccups of breath, way too loudly for Mother's taste. She shot a dagger glare at me. But how could I stop crying when I didn't even know how I had started? It had just come over me.

I stared for a long time at the wreaths of flowers wearing messages and posed on wobbly legs. Then I pushed my eyes toward the coffin. Old Thomas had become a gray clay man, his skin wrinkled crisp like dried roses. His cheeks were powdered and his white eye was sewn shut, and I thought it must have kept popping open, scaring unsuspecting folks. Old Thomas's hands were molded across the satin sheet wrapping him up as if he had just lain down for a nap. In his hands was his worn-down Bible, opened to the book of John. Across his chest lay a blue satin ribbon like he was the ambassador of something. He was silent now, no longer humming. Under his arm was Reddaddy's cane, tied with a little red velvet bag. That was from me; I'd sent it with Mammyrosy when the funeral home had taken his body away in the black Cadillac. In the bag I had put a barbecue rib, some dog leaf wafers, and the mustard seed he had once given me.

Then, I don't know why, I fell right down on my knees, right there on the whitest carpet strip I'd stepped on since I was a flower girl in a huge wedding. I held on to Old Thomas's death box, and, between crying wheezes, sniffs, and humming, I felt an awful pain in my knee, and I looked down and saw it was bleeding just like at confirmation. And right then the rocks rolled out, right through the closed-up skin, making three perfect red circles in a triangle on the white rug. I let go of the casket and tried to stretch over my kneecap so I could see what was going on, and Mother reached out to lift me up and get me out of there.

I pulled my arm from Mother's clutches and noticed that my knee had stopped bleeding and what remained were three white pin dots, like tiny freckles. I was embarrassed to have bloodied the church's rug, but at the same time I was awed by what had happened, and as I was staring, I heard sentences coming from the choir—"Bless you, sister," "Yes, Lord," "Praise Him"—as if those women understood what was going on.

Mother was humiliated beyond her patience. "All that carrying on—you should be ashamed," she whispered fiercely as she pulled me back toward our pew. "Excuse us; we can't stay," she mumbled to Mammyrosy, and we passed the pew and headed back up the aisle toward the front door. I could see Daddy and Sheriff Ferget had their arms across their chests and were paying no attention to us. I stopped to look for Mr. Washington, but he was no longer in the back.

We had barely passed under the EXIT sign, when I whooped one more heaving weep and yelled, "I've got to see Old Thomas one more time."

I tore away from Mother's grip, ran back to the altar area, reached in my pocket, and tossed two handfuls of dog leaves over Old Thomas's gray body. As I did, each dog leaf turned into a pink butterfly, and each butterfly lit on his head to form a circle where Old Thomas's gray ring of hair had once been. When the pink butterflies danced across his eyes and his mouth, I was sure I saw Old Thomas smile.

A white-robed soloist, her eyes closed, her arms uplifted and her body swaying, started bellowing "One More River to Cross," and that's when I saw Old Thomas, looking comfortable and golden, lifting up out of that metal box, carried along by a multitude of white airmail birds and a swarm of pink butterflies. They floated him along the white carpet, which waved like shiny ribbon candy. His white eye popped open as his face gleamed in a halo of rainbow colors, and for a second he glanced back and looked straight at me. A gold-glitter smile lit up his face, and he stood upright, and suddenly it was as if the church roof had dissolved and a wide river washed down over the whole congregation without getting anyone wet. A gentle whirlpool formed at the steeple, and Old Thomas walked toward the river.

The waters opened as he reached the sky and waved, and there, perched behind giant pearl gates, I saw Reddaddy with his beautifully combed red hair dozing on a carved silver stump. Reddaddy stood, and the two heaven-sent old friends embraced each other with a hug that made their hearts glow red, and then they turned and, arm in arm, wandered off into the deep blue.

III
Close Encounters

Twenty-Three

~~~

A year after Old Thomas's funeral, when I was sixteen, Sheriff
Ferget got permission from the highway patrol for me to have
a special permit to drive a car. In those days, sixteen-year-olds who
lived far out in the county could get such permits to drive to school,
to church, and to the grocery store, which happened to be close to
school. Daddy bought me a yellow Chevrolet convertible with a
black top and tail fins, and finally with that car I became popular
in school, since other girls couldn't drive for another year. Even the
boys began to take notice—of the car, not me.

High school and the advent of sorority rush life drew me away
from the farm, though Indio had become my best friend ever since
I'd lost Sweet Potato. Whenever he was grazing in the front pasture
and I wanted to ride, he wouldn't even lift his head as I grabbed a
lock of mane and pulled myself up. Sometimes he'd whinny, a non-
chalant hello, and I'd stretch out on his back, round as it was, and
watch clouds moving through the sky, wondering who was up there
and whether they were paying attention. I don't think anyone else
could see Indio and me but Mr. Washington, who, if he passed on
his way to his tree house, would lift up his dark glasses and smile
at us. Joseph, his hair reflecting the sun like a multicarat diamond,
paid us no mind.

One Saturday morning when I opened my dresser drawer, looking for some socks, I pulled out a pair I hadn't seen in a long time, unfolded them, stuck my hand into the heel, and found a collection of dog leaves, the very leaves I had gathered up after Old Thomas's body was carried off to the funeral home. In another sock I found beechos I'd gathered during the last visit to the Lolololo tree. I knew at once I had to take them out to Bozos and visit the elderly sisters.

I figured no one would know the difference if I drove up the highway in the opposite direction from school, now that it was paved all the way. Bozos wasn't one of the three designated places on my restricted license, but I was driving well by then, and the highway didn't scare me, even though Mother worried about the "evil roadhouses where men stopped to dance and dally with loose women." She worried especially about a place called Dew-Drop Inn that was near the highway turnoff to our road, but I drove past it all the time, and it never bothered me.

So I motored out the farm gate and cruised down the highway toward Bozos, which was still on isolated, undeveloped county land. Once I was near, I could smell that familiar pork crusting in the smoky pit, and as I drove up, I saw the small wooden building surrounded with trucks and automobiles bearing out-of-town license plates. I tried to hide my yellow convertible under the trees.

When the door slammed behind me, I saw Miss Irma. She was bent over, no longer able to stand up straight, but without even looking, she shot up and turned and at the sight of me shouted, "Lordy, lordy, Missy," and everyone in the place turned to look. Miss Irma hurried over and embraced me, all the while calling to Miss Lula. I was already taller than she was.

A moment later, the door with the creak swung open and there was Miss Lula, thinner than ever, her hair a mess of wisps, her hands red from barbecue sauce. She, too, hurried over to hug me.

"Oh, my child. It's been so long. You've grown up. A young lady. Yes, you are. How glad we are to see you." Miss Irma and Miss Lula smelled so good—like that delicious barbecue sauce. Each one grabbed an arm and pulled me back through the squeaking door to the kitchen.

"Come on, get that wooden spoon and stir up those beans," Miss Irma said. Miss Lula shook her head. "A young lady you are," she said. "You look just like your grandfather. His eyes. His smile. Yes, you are his blood all the way."

"Tell us what you're up to, dear," Miss Lula said, and as I began to stir the browning beans, I told them about my driving license.

"Have you got any beechos?" I asked the sisters.

"We've had to make do without the beechos," Miss Lula said, and I heard the sadness in her lilt. "Ever since Old Thomas departed . . ."

That was my chance. I reached into my bag and said, "Look what I've brought you," and I pulled out the sock and unrolled them on the kitchen counter so that they could see those beechos and dog leaves.

Miss Lula began to weep, and Miss Irma put her hand on Miss Lula's shoulder. "Now there, sister," she said, but I could tell the sight of those beechos moved her almost to tears.

"How about two Dr. Peppers and a root beer?" One of the customers had peered over the door top and was shouting.

"Coming right up," Miss Irma said.

I noticed that though the place was busy, the sisters now had a helper—a woman with her hair dyed yellow in a beehive hairdo, wearing too much makeup and go-go boots. "Natsy," Miss Lulu said to her, "did you take the order on the window table?"

"Yes, Miss Irma," she said in a high squeal.

"Miss Lula, still got those pennies in your shoes?" I laughed.

"Pennies aren't good for much else nowadays," she said. "I don't even know if there is magic left in beechos now that Old Thomas has passed. Take a bite of these ribs, Missy. See if you remember."

I held two ribs between my fingers and with delicacy bit into the famous Bozos specialty, drenched in red sauce. The moment I did my heart began to race, and a moment later my feet had lifted up off the ground. I closed my eyes and tried to feel the magic. I did a somersault in the air and landed on the floor again.

"Haven't lost your touch, Miss Lula," I said. She had been paying no attention.

"Natsy, take over. I'm going on a break," Miss Irma said from the next room, and once again she pushed through the musical door, stopped and looked at me, and said, "Missy, we got some catching up to do."

She reached out for a plate and packed it with ribs and beans, and the three of us pulled stools up to the counter, where Miss Lula and I could pick at the meat that had already been chopped for sandwiches. I liked the crusty dark edges where the sauce had burned in.

"There's not been nor will there be a pair like your Reddaddy and Old Thomas," Miss Irma said. "And we can throw in Sheriff Ferget, too, since he went on expeditions with his old friends. Did you ever hear about that bear trip?"

"No, Miss Irma," I said, and I knew I didn't have to beg for her to tell me.

"Lordy, that story was so typical of those two old coots. Only Sheriff Ferget, who was there with them, can really tell it like it was," she added, wiping the grease off her hands onto her apron.

Miss Lula said softly, "It was the only time Reddaddy tried to take Old Thomas on a hunting trip."

"The first and the last," roared Miss Irma. "Yep, Old Thomas'd be the first to admit he was no hunter. He was a healer, and he couldn't kill any animal, even though it might make good eating."

Miss Irma went on to tell me the story of the time the three men went down to Wilson's plantation. She told the story the way I liked stories—the way Reddaddy and Old Thomas and the sheriff always told me, so I could see it all as clearly as if I'd been there. She said they all saddled up and rode for two hours into the Ozarks, looking for deer. When they came upon a huge herd of white-tails grazing high up above that rocky timberline, Reddaddy acknowledged that they were already a bit farther up the mountains than they'd normally go, but the deer stools were fresh.

Just as they began to talk about the sheriff's desire to go on because he hadn't gotten a decent rack of horns to hang at the station and brag about, Sheriff Ferget banged through the door of Bozos and headed right into the kitchen. Without even a word, he picked himself out a big chunk of meat well soaked in sauce, and that's when he noticed the three of us sitting there.

"Missy, what are you doing out here? It's off your route," he said, more surprised than reproving. Miss Irma pulled up another stool, but the sheriff had put on so much weight, he couldn't get comfortable on it.

"Oh, Sheriff Ferget. I couldn't see much difference in going ten miles west or going ten miles east on the same highway," I said, but then I quickly added, "The real reason I came here is to bring special gifts to Miss Lula and Miss Irma. I haven't seen them in such a long time."

"Rules is rules, Missy," he said casually as he bit off a big chaw of pork. "Are you ladies getting into mischief telling stories?"

"We'd just got into rememberin' about that time you three went hunting on horseback over in the Ozarks."

Settling on the stool as best he could, the sheriff took over, and I liked that because, in truth, he told stories best. After all, he had been there. He said he remembered Old Thomas was antsy and sore in his saddle, on the back of a horse he'd never met. I already knew Old Thomas had never taken to riding.

"His horse had the ugliest face I ever saw," the sheriff continued. "Her ears bent in a fold. Her lower lip hung about two inches farther down than the rest of her mouth, and it was covered in white whiskers. Odd for a black horse. She had blue eyes that remained half closed most of the time. One eye was blue. The other wasn't there."

He went on to tell how they reached a clearing right above the timberline where a hundred deer, some with antlers bigger than the governor's chandelier, stood there looking so beautiful, the sheriff lost all his hunting desire.

Their horses, spooked by something, began to turn in circles in the deep snow, and all of a sudden Old Thomas's ugly mare lurched out as if she were running out of a rodeo chute. They yelled at Old Thomas to pull back on the reins, but they were already halfway across the snowbanks and heading into a clearing. The strangest thing was, the old mare didn't sink into the snow—she seemed to skate along over the top—and the other two horses continued to twist in circles before taking off downhill.

Meanwhile, Old Thomas's horse was making a beeline for the

herd, trotting straight up the rocky cliff, when they suddenly heard a roar, as if the faucets had been turned off, and Old Thomas and his mare were high up on the other side of the clearing, in front of a huge tree and staring straight into the face of a bear. She was a mama bear standing on her two legs, with two cubs feeding beside her.

That bear pulled down a large branch of berries and, grabbing a bunch in her paws, quickly passed them to her cubs before pulling off a few for herself. Old Thomas's horse found a lower branch, meanwhile, and began to snap berries off with her teeth. Everybody was groaning with what sounded like delight, except Reddaddy couldn't decide if the noises were good or bad. All of a sudden they heard Old Thomas humming, and the ugly old mare's folded-up ears straightened and turned back toward where Old Thomas's sound was coming from. That old bear was moaning and Old Thomas was humming and the old horse was chewing, all in the same key. Old Thomas's hair turned snow white, and his mouth puckered like a hungry manta ray's lips, and a weird whiteness surrounded the scene as if it had been cut out of a tea doily.

Now, Reddaddy and Sheriff Ferget, having lost them, didn't have any horses or any guns, and they didn't know what to do, until all of a sudden Old Thomas's mare turned her tail side toward the bear and headed straight down, back toward them, with Old Thomas holding tightly to the saddle horn. When they reached the far side of the clearing, Old Thomas looked at his friends and asked them why they were hiding in the bush, but before they could answer, Sheriff Ferget saw those two bear cubs behind Old Thomas. He shouted at him to watch out, but Old Thomas knew what was going on. What he knew that no one else did was that Mama Bear was wounded and dying. She had given her cubs to Old Thomas to take care of.

"Yes, Lord," Miss Irma said when the story was finished. "It sure must have been a strange group slipping and sliding straight down that mountain: two sad old deer hunters on foot, a colored man on a flop-eared ugly horse, and two bear cubs playing with branches along the way. Just to think, now those cubs are grown and are popular attractions at the zoo. Fine fellow, Mr. Red. Always thinking about giving delight to others."

I'd never heard that story, but it didn't surprise me a bit. I knew Old Thomas always understood things the way no one else did—the way I wanted to understand them, too.

And after the story was finished and Sheriff Ferget was full, he forgot all about my driving off-limits.

Twenty - Four

Sometimes Daddy let me drive the few miles down to Hopper's General Store for soda pop, but that was about as daring as I was allowed to get. I knew if anything happened to the car, my driving privileges would be over, so I spent most of my free time locked up in my room, listening to rhythm-and-blues music. I tried to invent dances, or at least do the ones I saw the kids at school doing, but I couldn't move the way the popular girls did, like molasses poured over pancakes. I did know every song on the hit parade, from the Platters to the Drifters, and when I read in the paper there was a concert of the most popular rhythm-and-blues groups coming to the auditorium on Beale Street, I was sad because I knew there'd be no way my parents would let me go. Blacks and whites never attended public events together, and the adults I knew said black music like Elvis's was evil. If someone like me were seen at such a thing downtown, it would be a scandal.

But I couldn't get the idea out of my mind, and one day when I was visiting the barn, I asked Mr. Washington if he knew anything about rhythm and blues.

"Well, Missy," he said—he was wearing his dark glasses, so I couldn't see his eyes—"you just haven't been in the right place at the right time. You don't come down to the barn anymore, and I understand that perfectly, but if you did, you might hear some of that music that's turning your insides around."

"Then why don't you ever play the radio?" I asked.

He smiled. "Remember your mother's mare Betsy Dare? I'm obliged to keep a radio tuned to rhythm-and-blues music in her stall, or else she'll jump up on the tailboards and bang herself up. Her favorite singer is Bo Diddley."

Just the sound of his name excited me—he was one of the musicians who was going to be playing at the auditorium—and I was so excited I asked Mr. Washington if he'd heard about the concert, and if he was going.

"I might if I had a dance partner to go with me," he said.

I looked away so he wouldn't think I was interested—that would have embarrassed me—and I turned the tables on him.

"I'm sure you wouldn't have any trouble finding someone to dance with, Mr. Washington. Don't you have lots of girlfriends?"

The minute the question was out of my mouth, I blushed with embarrassment. Mr. Washington's life wasn't any of my business. He was much older than I and had been a whole bunch more places than I'd ever even dreamed of going to. But when he laughed I felt better, and he said, "You don't see them climbing up into my tree house, do you?"

"No." I laughed with him, but I was sure I sounded silly.

"Maybe if you just go on and go to the concert, you'll meet someone there," I said, trying to sound confident. "Mother says if I go out with even an ugly boy I don't like, he might have attractive friends I'd like better. That's what she says, anyway. Of course, she won't let me go out on a date with anybody, unless it's at a chaperoned society event at the club."

I was just about to turn away, when Mr. Washington took off those glasses and looked me straight in the eye with a look so strong, even Indio stopped grazing and raised his head. "I'm waiting for you to go with me, Missy," he said.

I couldn't let Mr. Washington see my face—I'm sure it had turned as red as a tomato—so I quickly turned around on Indio's withers so I was sitting backward across him. In the silence of the barn, I rubbed Indio's strange patterns of hair and bent over to lie on his back, my chin digging into his rump bone, arms draped over the sides of his hips. He liked that, and it gave me a sense of comfort and some time to think about how to answer.

Finally I said, "I've never gone anywhere with any boy, Mr. Washington. My parents won't allow it."

"You should try it. You might like it," he said. "Why don't you put on your courage and accompany me down to the auditorium, see what it's like?"

I couldn't think of a word to say. This idea was the worst thing I could ever do in the eyes of my parents, but in my view it sounded too wonderful even to imagine.

"Missy, you're becoming a beautiful young lady," Mr. Washington went on. "Don't be afraid to trust yourself, just like that night riding Sweet Potato in the pasture. You may have your heart broken a few times, but you'll break a lot of hearts, too. Mine might be your first."

My heart was thudding in my ears as he talked. I wanted so much to find out all about him—like why his eyes were so strange and about the magic he could do and how he knew so many things.

"You really think I'm ready to be a grown-up?" I finally managed.

"There's no better way to find out than to do something you want to do."

"But . . ."

"Think of it. You could get those singers' autographs for your collection."

That took my breath away. I had never mentioned my collection to him, or to anyone else, for that matter. "How do you know about that?" I asked. "How do you know what people want when they don't even know it themselves?"

"Secrets, Missy. Secrets and insight," and as he said this he walked around Indio and came close and said, very softly, "I'll wait for you down at the barn Saturday night. Your parents go out to play bridge until almost one. We'll go downtown, take a peek, and be back before anyone knows what's going on."

I looked him right in the eye and shook my head, searching for every reason I could find to stomp down temptation. "But everyone knows my car, and I don't have a permit to drive at night, much less all the way downtown."

"I know the back roads well, Missy." He put his hand around my calf, and my whole body turned warm.

"What about Mammyrosy? She won't let me near the back door when she's babysitting."

"She'll be sound asleep before *The Amos 'n Andy Show* is halfway through."

"You're right about that." I had to laugh. He seemed to know everything about everyone. I was sure he knew that Robertelee fell asleep on the floor right beside her.

"Are you convinced?" he asked as he released my leg.

"I'm thinking about it," I said as I slid off Indio. "Either I'll be there or I won't. I just don't know."

As quickly as I could, I ran from the barn and back to my bicycle, my heart beating so fast I thought it might fly through my chest. I didn't know if I could do it, but I'd been sneaking away all my life, and I couldn't imagine passing up this chance—I hoped I could find the courage. And then I did.

I dressed in my favorite poodle skirt made of red felt because it had a lot of swirl, and I wore a white shirt tied at the waist, with the collar up around my neck, and white socks and brown-and-white saddle shoes. I'd cut my hair short, and I brushed it back in an Elvis ducktail, the look that had become so popular because of Elvis Presley. Even he was supposed to be there that night—I kept getting chills just thinking about all the people I was going to see. I figured Elvis was just a rumor, but who knew what kind of magic might happen? And thankfully Mammyrosy and Robertelee fell asleep, just like Mr. Washington predicted.

As we left the farm, Mr. Washington didn't say much, and I thought maybe he was as scared as I was, and I couldn't help but wonder what would happen if we were discovered in the same car together, or if someone found out I'd left the house without permission. Still, I reasoned, I couldn't see much harm in going to hear good music, even though I knew "Work with Me Annie" was a far cry from the Lester Lanin music the bands played at formal dances at the country clubs. My favorite song was Johnny Ace's 'Pledging My Love.'" I had it on a 45. He wouldn't be there, though. He'd just been accidentally killed by a pistol shot down in Houston, Texas.

But as we began to drive along those empty back roads—Mr. Washington telling me which turns to take—I began to feel at ease, and I stopped feeling shy or afraid. It was like the night in the pasture with Sweet Potato—we were sailing along, and everything seemed to be right, and then, before I knew it, we were parking my yellow convertible four blocks down a side street in someone's driveway. Mr. Washington paid the man twenty-five cents and led me down toward the club, and we heard the crowds and the crazy beat even before we saw the crowds pushing their way inside. People crowded outside the New Daisy, waiting to squeeze in to join the others on the dance floor; there was no room to sit or stand, which was no surprise, since this was the first time some of these great rhythm-and-blues recording artists were performing in Memphis. Most of the people were black, but sprinkled in were some white people, and outside policemen wearing helmets and swinging black batons rode past on their big brown horses.

We stood outside for a moment, and all of a sudden I felt Mr. Washington's arm around my waist and he whispered, "Over here—I know some folks," and he practically lifted me up off the ground and pulled me around the corner and inside through a door marked No ENTRANCE.

Nate Williams, the man who ran WDIA, Memphis's first all-black radio station, was the commentator that night, and he had the packed crowd cheering in anticipation of what was to come, but the place was so noisy and smoky, I began to feel like I couldn't breathe, and when I looked around, I realized it was so gray and shadowy, I couldn't see a thing except onstage, where two spotlights hovered. I kept my head lowered—I didn't want anyone I might know to see me—and when I saw some white teenagers, boys and girls, passing cigarettes, I worried I might recognize one of them. Even from a few feet away I could smell the girls' hairspray, and the boys were dressed in pink-and-black Elvis shirts from Lansky Bros on Beale Street, but mostly it was the black teenagers who owned this place, and over the recorded music piped in over big speakers, I couldn't hear a thing until Mr. Washington moved in close and whispered, right in my ear, "Cheer up, sweet virgin. You're gonna be all right."

I turned to look at him, and his smile was so handsome and kind, I had to smile back.

"Don't be afraid," he said. "Everyone's happy tonight. Everyone. Especially me," and I began to feel so at ease with him—he was so big and strong, I knew no one would harm me as long as he was at my side—I almost forgot how defiant I was being, how horrified Mother would be if she knew where I was and whom I was with.

Finally the first group walked onstage, a local group, Rufus and Bones, come to warm up for the Five Satins, and once they began to play and the beat took hold, the whole place began to shake and move. It seemed like every person found a partner and began to dance, and I could feel the rhythms in my body, and even I felt like I could dance. I was holding my autograph book, just like everyone was, and suddenly I felt Mr. Washington grab it out of my hand and he disappeared behind a curtain, but before I could miss him, he was back at my side and the pages of my book were filled with autographs from everyone, with a special message from Fats Domino, just for me. *For Sara*, it said.

I couldn't believe my eyes. "Mr. Washington, how can I thank you?"

"Only the best for my moon frog virgin," he said, and he touched my shoulder, and I felt a shiver run through me. "Do you feel better now?" he asked.

I wanted to sound hip, so I shouted back, over the music, "Really cool."

"Well," he laughed, "you're better off than me. The heat in here is getting to my soul," and with that he lifted me up by the waist and carried me to a side table, where he stood me up so I could see over the crowds.

Up there the unfamiliar smell of what Mr. Washington explained was "loco weed" filled my nostrils, and I began to feel a little dizzy, but the music was like a balm to my soul, and I stood there mesmerized as Mr. Washington moved out into the crowd, mixing and moving with the dancers as the music got as hot as the building. I couldn't take my eyes away from him as black women thrust their body parts at him in some sort of trance, until Mr. Washington began doing things that made all his muscles double in size. Sweat poured off him, and pretty soon I had to look away. I didn't want to see him doing those things. I felt the same way I felt when I watched tango dancers in the movies—there was more going on than I knew about, but I knew enough to know that, and I wasn't ready to think about Mr. Washington that way.

And then all of a sudden he was right in front of me, looking right at me. He'd taken off his glasses, and I could see deep into those emerald eyes that locked my own so I couldn't look anywhere else. Hank Ballard and the Midnighters began to sing "Annie Had a Baby," and Mr. Washington grabbed my waist and slid me off the table. He reached out and placed his hands on my hips and pushed them, gently, trying to get me to dance. I could feel the movement he wanted me to make, but I was afraid to free my body into his hands, and with that music grinding and the crowd singing along and Mr. Washington seeming transformed by ecstasy, I couldn't tell any longer if he knew I was there. Everyone around us was hot and sweaty, and the smell of all that skin and sweat mixed with weed and alcohol gathered in my head, and I began to worry again—I worried that I was seeing things I shouldn't be seeing, feeling things I shouldn't be feeling. I was worried that I would turn into one of those girls I could see who were falling onto the floor and making rubbery moves, touching their partners everywhere.

Now that the music was cresting in electric waves, it all became too much, and I pulled away from Mr. Washington and ran out the side door into the night air. Outside, a ring of police with billy clubs and groups of white adults with hate in their faces were surrounding the building, but I brushed past them and ran up the side street, looking for my car.

I didn't for one moment worry about Mr. Washington. He seemed to know lots of people, and I knew he could find his way home. And I figured I could, too. Linden to Third to Union Avenue, where my school was located. That led to Highway 72. I decided I would drive right down the highway, where I would be safe. I was sure I would. Once inside the car, I opened all the windows and let the wind blow everything away—the sweat and music and loco weed. I supposed I wasn't in any danger.

It wasn't yet midnight by the time I reached home, and the house was dark but for the single light in the den, where Mammyrosy and Robertelee were sound asleep, looking like beached whales on the Persian carpet. The television across the room was bright with Fred Astaire and Ginger Rogers dancing properly in black and white, in gowns and tails. I quickly ran up to my room, where I threw myself onto the bed and looked over my autograph book. Mr. Washington had gotten me all the best. He really had watched out for me. I felt sorry for not having said good-bye, and I wondered whom he was dancing with, and who was playing now, and who would drive him home, and what we would say to each other when we next saw each other.

I fell asleep thinking about him, but a few hours later I woke up in a sweat, with one thought pounding through my head. What if the girls of Sigma Kappa Sigma sorority found out where I had been? Mother had pulled strings to get me into that sorority, and just a few weeks earlier I'd been initiated as a pledge. I had to keep a cigar box filled with candy and gum to offer to the seniors at school who made us get on our knees in reverence, and if they didn't like what I had to offer, I could be removed from the list of candidates for membership. Most of them were nice to me but mean to the more popular girls, and all I could think about was whether one of them was at the club that night—or someone else whom someone knew. What if word got out? I stayed awake all night worrying about that.

The next evening I was up in my bedroom, recording my latest experiences in my diary and resting up, and Mother was in her dressing room, getting ready for dinner, when I felt the energy in the house begin to change. The dogs began to bark at the stirred-up atmosphere, and then Daddy called up to me to come down to the den to talk to him.

Daddy seldom showed his anger to me, but I sensed what was coming as I sat down across from him and looked into his angry eyes.

"What in the world did you think you were doing?" Daddy sounded like blinds rattling when a storm hit.

"What are you talking about, Daddy?" I said, feigning innocence. I suspected he knew.

"You know damn well what I'm talking about! Shut up, dogs." The dogs immediately obeyed, and I realized I was doomed. He did know.

I lowered my head and said nothing, and he roared on.

"Whatever possessed you to take off in your car and drive all the way downtown to Beale Street for a music show that the whole town has been upset about?"

I looked up. I needed to know how he'd found out. "Who's upset, Daddy?"

"The censors, the white-rights groups, the politicians, the police department, the schools. That kind of music is evil, and it's influencing the minds of our young people to do evil things."

That was too much. This wasn't Mother talking, this was Daddy, and the words he was saying sounded ridiculous to me, and I said so. "Daddy, good music is good music. There are more people than just Vaughn Monroe who can sing." Vaughn Monroe was the big-band singer Daddy loved most, but that just seemed to enrage him still more, and his face got still redder. "Listen, young lady, you aren't even old enough to be in an establishment that allows liquor through the door, much less music of the vulgar kind. You just turned sixteen. You have to be twenty-one to drink liquor."

Daddy was the man who had always been understanding, and I couldn't believe he had lost all his senses. "I don't drink liquor, Daddy," I argued. "I don't even like the smell. I'm just like other teenagers—I want to start learning about life. Is that such a sin?"

"Don't you sass me, young lady. You violated our trust and sneaked away knowing full well that an earthquake couldn't move Mammyrosy from sleep. Not only that, you violated the law of the state of Tennessee and could have gotten Sheriff Ferget in heaps of trouble. Use your head for something besides keeping your ears apart, daughter."

The thought that I had hurt the sheriff suddenly weighed on me—I hadn't thought about that. "Yes, Daddy," I said softly.

"I guess I should have seen it coming. Who put you up to this? Washington?"

I looked up fast. "No, Daddy, no. He had nothing to do with it." I was relieved to know Daddy seemed not to know for sure who had been with me. Obviously someone knew I'd been there, but maybe no one had actually seen me. I steered the conversation toward my classmates and explained that everyone had been talking about the revue.

"If your mother's friends finds out, you'll be a scandal," he said when I stopped talking, and I felt relief flood through me when I realized Mother didn't yet know.

"Daddy, all my favorites were performing. I saw Fats Domino and the Five Satins . . ."

He shook his head, but I could see that some of my excitement had seeped into him. "Missy, I think you've lost your senses," he said. "You headed right down into the middle of the darkies' town. You could have been raped or robbed. Anything might have happened to you."

"Oh, Daddy, people weren't trying to do bad things, and there were other white people enjoying it, too, and there were lots of police."

He leaned forward. "I've made a decision," he said. "No more driving for the whole summer."

"Don't be cruel, Daddy. At least I confessed."

He had picked up his newspaper—I knew he was dismissing me. I had wanted to make my point to him, wanted to convince him to see things my way, but I'd been wrong to try. He was finished with me, except for one more thing. "Your grandfather and Old Thomas will rip up the clouds of heaven when they find out about this." He looked over at the portrait of Reddaddy hanging over the fireplace, and I saw my opening. He'd always said I took after my grandfather, so maybe we could have a real conversation. I needed to know how he'd found out. And so I asked.

He shook his head again.

"Your pal Sheriff Ferget saw you go there, and he kept his mouth shut until I confirmed it with him. He followed you home to make sure you were safe. It's just a good thing you left before the riots started."

I'd heard nothing about the riots, but now he explained the police had stormed the place when the dancing grew more heated, and I realized how lucky I was to have left when I had, and I realized he was right. I was lucky to have Sheriff Ferget. He was one of my angels, I supposed.

"You're lucky, and you know Sheriff Ferget could have taken away your special license," Daddy said.

I nodded, and I looked over at Reddaddy's portrait and I knew there were more people looking after me than even Daddy realized. I could feel Mr. Washington pressing on my heart, and I stuck my hand into the pocket of my jeans and rubbed the stone frog I always kept there.

Twenty-Five

It was that very night Frightnin' collapsed, and I couldn't help thinking maybe that was my punishment for breaking all the rules, though even Daddy said probably he was ready to be with Old Thomas again. Still, the mood in the house was heavy all night and into the morning, and I decided I needed to go to the Lolololo tree. I knew it was the only place that would make me feel all right.

Mammyrosy usually didn't pay much attention anymore to all the passing through the kitchen we did, but that morning she stopped me, and she knew just by looking at me where I was headed. I saw that in her eyes. "Missy, where you think you goin'?" she asked. "Out to that tree?"

I didn't like to hurt anyone, but especially not Mammyrosy, and I'd hurt her by sneaking out on her, and I could see all that hurt in her eyes. So I didn't just run.

I looked at her with all the love I felt and said, "I just need to go somewhere where I can think about all this, Mammyrosy. I sure will be glad when school's out for summer."

Mammyrosy shook her head, and I saw a little lift at the corners of her mouth, like she was fighting off a smile. "What in the world are you going to do with yourself then? No school. Mischief on your shoulder. Breasts bulging. Mm-mmm. I'm worried to death, young'un."

But I had to get to that tree. I had to lay it all out for Old Thomas—everything that had happened. As I was standing there, I could smell Mammyrosy's biscuits, but I also thought I could still smell the sweet smoke smell that had been so thick inside that place. At the time I had no idea what loco weed, as Mr. Washington had called it, was, but I had begun to feel as if my body were like a window screen, and things I didn't know were getting in through the holes. And that song, the one Fats Domino sang—"Ain't That a Shame"—was playing over and over in my head, and I couldn't forget how strange I had felt watching Mr. Washington dance to that powerful beat with all those women reaching at him like he was the last chocolate bonbon in the box. I could still almost see the outline of hair and heads moving up and down in a sensual séance and curtained by that halo of smoke that still seemed to be choking me.

I had to get out and breathe fresh air, so I said that, and I saw Mammyrosy soften, and I knew she understood everything in that moment. So I just promised her I wouldn't be all day.

The grass around the Lolololo tree was green as spinach, set off from the timothy weeds and other long, clinging stalks that normally grew in the pasture. No one mowed here, so the Lolololo area stayed untouched and undiscovered, and for a minute it seemed as if the Lolololo tree's crossbars curved forward to embrace me like an old friend.

I hadn't been here in too long, but a hodgepodge of animals still called this tree home. Airmail birds still occupied a few nests, and snakes popped in and out of their O-holes. A multiplicity of ladybugs rested on the trunk so that it looked almost like Christmas, but the leaves were scarce on the branches, the dog wafers all gone. Still, it smelled good here—clean, fresh, untainted.

I found my favorite stump and pushed it up against the tree so I could lean back. Funny how whenever I did that, the bark turned as soft as Mother's goose-down pillows. I tossed off my shoes and unbuttoned my shirt and breathed with the pleasure of being in my own private spot, alone and free in the place Old Thomas had left for me. Quickly, a gaggle of red and yellow ladybugs began to crawl over my white bra, making a soundless flitter as they arrived, tickling me. I reached into my pocket for my frog stone and laid it in the middle of my belly, on my bellybutton. It balanced there, looking straight at me.

As I leaned back into the folds of the tree, I felt as if I could stay forever, but I also missed Frightnin'. He had always accompanied me just so he could get away from the pack of new dogs my parents adored. He'd howl and gripe every time they started tugging on his ears and tail when he was trying to rest. The four puppies had taken over Daddy's lap and the house, and I thought Daddy might not even notice he was gone. But out here at the Lolololo, it seemed he had to be present, and I reached my hand out on my left side to pet him. I felt his memory there, and it comforted me.

I couldn't help but doze off. A breeze smelling like damask roses picked up, and I heard tinkling sounds, like crystal wind chimes, but I paid them little mind, just kept on with my dozing. Then something wet my foot. I jerked it back and opened my eyes, and there was Joseph, his hair so mirrorlike all I could see was me.

"How did you know I was here?" I whispered, as I sat up and quickly buttoned my shirt. The ladybugs flew away, but the stone frog stayed where it was, and I heard his voice before I saw him— Mr. Washington.

"Ain't that a shame," he said. "You deserted me, young lady."

I couldn't look at him, so I looked everywhere else. "I got scared," I said. "I just got scared. What if someone I knew had seen us there?"

"I doubt your society pals would have been at such a gig," Washington said, and I finally looked up and saw that his shirt was open, revealing glistening black skin. "Don't be paranoid," he said, as Joseph circled me and finally decided to lie down right in Frightnin's old place.

"Why are you so afraid of me?" Washington asked. He moved nearer and sat on his haunches, like an Indian. He was chewing on a stalk of grass, and he snapped another from the weeds nearby and handed it to me. "Chew," he said.

I chewed. The flavor was like sweet milk, and I couldn't help but smile to discover that a weed could taste so good. I knew honeysuckle vines were sweet, but I'd never imagined the taste of weeds.

"You behave with me like you used to behave with Sweet Potato until you learned that she wasn't your enemy but the wind that could move you above the earth."

I looked at him and nodded. That was true.

"Let me be your wind, Sacred Virgin of the Moon Frog," he said very softly, and then he stood and walked to the other side of the Lolololo. I stayed where I was. I could hear him singing Elvis's "Don't Be Cruel," and when the song was finished, he was silent, and so was I. I wondered if he had gone away as suddenly as he had appeared, and when I thought he was gone, I suddenly missed him terribly.

"Mr. Washington . . . ," I finally called, and a second later he was right in front of me again—though I hadn't seen him walk there.

"How did you find the Lolololo tree?" I asked.

"I always know where you are, Missy," he said. "I sense your presence, and all I have to do is go there. It doesn't matter where you are—I can be there. It's old Indian wisdom that latched onto my spirit. You have been sent to me. I wish you could believe that."

My hair began to swirl and twist, until a crown of rose petals of all hues of red and purple formed upon it, and before I could comprehend what could be happening, Mr. Washington took my hand with such gentleness I didn't even know I had risen up from the earth.

He put his fingers in my back and pulled me so close to him I wondered if I'd come out the other side. The stone frog stayed right in place, pressing itself into the muscles of his stomach.

"I'll always be your wind, Missy. It's who I am," he said, and he touched my face and pressed his lips on mine. I had never been kissed, and for one moment I was so worried about what I should be doing that the moment almost missed me. In an instant, golden ladybugs tangled in my hair and crawled inside the pocket of my white shirt. When I moved, they swarmed away to the trunk of the Lolololo tree. There was nothing more of me, because I had become something of a new place and a new feeling, and I knew I would never again be afraid of Mr. Washington, and I did not want whatever he was doing to me to end.

Then I forgot everything—who I was, who Mr. Washington was, where we were—and I became the earth and the trees and the lady-bugs and the tangled grass stalks and the green snakes as he and I were plaited together into a form that was new and more powerful than the romance comics I had read and reread, wondering if that would ever happen to me. I just gave up what I had been to become what I was now, and, at once, I knew I was better than any of those stories. I was the story.

Acknowledgments

About the Author

©LOU

Reverend Audrey Taylor Gonzalez was born in Memphis, Tennessee in 1939. In the span of her long life, she's been a journalist, TV host, art gallery owner, racehorse breeder, mountain climber, world traveler, breast cancer survivor, and the first woman to be ordained to holy orders in the Southern Cone of South America at Uruguay's Holy Trinity Cathedral in Montevideo. She is the author of three books, the fictional memoir *The Lolololo Tree* and two collections of writings and homilies, *Sermons and Such* and *The Shady Place*. *South of Everything* is her first novel. She resides in Memphis, Tennessee. For more about her, visit: www.audreytaylorgonzalez.org.

SELECTED TITLES FROM SHE WRITES PRESS

She Writes Press is an independent publishing company
founded to serve women writers everywhere.
Visit us at www.shewritespress.com.

The Outskirts of Hope: A Memoir by Jo Ivester
$16.95, 978-1-63152-964-1
A moving, inspirational memoir about how living and working in an
all-black town during the height of the civil rights movement pro-
foundly affected the author's entire family—and how they in turn
impacted the community.

Faint Promise of Rain by Anjali Mitter Duva
$16.95, 978-1-938314-97-1
Adhira, a young girl born to a family of Hindu temple dancers, is raised
to be dutiful—but ultimately, as the world around her changes, it is her
own bold choice that will determine the fate of her family and of their
tradition.

All the Light There Was by Nancy Kricorian
$16.95, 978-1-63152-905-4
A lyrical, finely wrought tale of loyalty, love, and the many faces of
resistance, told from the perspective of an Armenian girl living in Paris
during the Nazi occupation of the 1940s.

The Sweetness by Sande Boritz Berger
$16.95, 978-1-63152-907-8
A compelling and powerful story of two girls—cousins living on separate continents—whose strikingly different lives are forever changed
when the Nazis invade Vilna, Lithuania.

The Rooms Are Filled by Jessica Null Vealitzek
$16.95, 978-1-938314-58-2
The coming-of-age story of two outcasts—a nine-year-old boy who
just lost his father, and a closeted young woman—brought together by
circumstance.

The Belief in Angels by J. Dylan Yate
$16.95, 978-1-938314-64-3
From the Majdonek death camp to a volatile hippie household on the
East Coast, this narrative of tragedy, survival, and hope spans more
than fifty years, from the 1920s to the 1970s.